Advance praise for
A HIGHLY UNLIKELY SCENARIO

"Part Italo Calvino, part Ray Bradbury. In this extraordinary novel, Rachel Cantor explores questions of self-knowledge, true love, and family, all while saving the world—and winning readers—in the past, present, and future."
—HANNAH TINTI, AUTHOR OF *THE GOOD THIEF*

"A sharp, witty, and immensely entertaining debut."
—EMILY ST. JOHN MANDEL, AUTHOR OF *THE LOLA QUARTET*

"Cosmic and comic, full of philosophy, mysticism, and celestial whimsy. A story of listening, of souls and bodies, that is at once both profoundly wild and wildly profound."
—CHARLES YU, AUTHOR OF *HOW TO LIVE SAFELY IN A SCIENCE FICTIONAL UNIVERSE*

"I didn't know I needed a mystical Jewish Douglas Adams in my life, but Rachel Cantor is it. Buy this book, *bubeleh*! It will surprise you in ways large and small, and it will fill you with delight." **—EMILY BARTON, AUTHOR OF *BROOKLAND***

A HIGHLY UNLIKELY SCENARIO

OR, A _Neetsa Pizza_ EMPLOYEE'S
GUIDE TO SAVING THE WORLD

RACHEL CANTOR

MELVILLE HOUSE
BROOKLYN · LONDON

A HIGHLY UNLIKELY SCENARIO
OR, A NEETSA PIZZA EMPLOYEE'S
GUIDE TO SAVING THE WORLD

First Melville House printing: January 2014

The author gratefully acknolwedges the Millay Colony
for the Arts and the Hall Farm Center for their generous
support during the writing of this book.

Melville House Publishing   8 Blackstock Mews
     145 Plymouth Street   and   Islington
     Brooklyn, NY 11201   London N4 2BT

mhpbooks.com   facebook.com/mhpbooks   @melvillehouse

Library of Congress Cataloging-in-Publication Data

Cantor, Rachel.
  A highly unlikely scenario, or, a Neetsa Pizza employee's guide
to saving the world : a novel / Rachel Cantor.
     pages cm
  ISBN 978-1-61219-264-2
  I. Title.
  PS3603.A5877H54 2014
  813'.6—dc23
                                                    2013024566

Design by Christopher King

Printed in the United States of America
1 3 5 7 9 10 8 6 4 2

For Leah, Josh, Elena, and Cole, with love

PART ONE
THE WHITE ROOM

The missing complaints

Leonard's usual complaint volume was twelve calls per hour, his average dispatch time two-point-five minutes, but for three nights running, Leonard had received no complaints whatsoever. No cranks, no callers saying they'd ordered *super* not *supernal*, not even a wrong number.

Leonard wasn't worried, not at first—satellites blew up all the time, Neetsa Pizza always worked it out. He took time to catch up on the online antics of Sue & Susheela. And to ask questions of the Brazen Head:

Q: Are Sue & Susheela really twins? With each other, I mean.

A: They entered this world more or less at the same time and for the same purpose. Over and out!

By night two, Leonard would have welcomed even a crank. He was not always optimally compassionate with cranks, though on this matter, Neetsa Pizza was clear: all callers deserve the best, which is to say, a pizza shaped according to Pythagorean principles. In principle, though not always in practice, Leonard subscribed to this creed, which also stated:

Those who experience a rending of their joy are in pain.

Clients must be relieved of their pain. It is a sacred calling to restore clients to optimal satisfaction.

Pain is relieved through compassion. Compassion is best achieved in a White Room, and delivered through concentrated Listening, use of time-tested Listener algorithms, and liberal use of Neetsa Pizza coupons.

So Leonard listened in his White Room, ten hours per night, seven nights per week, ten being a perfect number, according to Pythagoras, seven being pure and inviolable, Leonard being, by trade and also by nature, a Listener.

Like most young men, Leonard had wanted to be a pizza thrower. He admired the gold braid, he wanted to toss pizzas in NP's zero-gravity rotating window. But eye-hand coordination wasn't Leonard's Special Gift, and he vomited when upside down. He begged then to be a pizza greeter, but he lacked the necessary ebullience. Pizza neatener? Alas, his examiners found, his love of order was not sufficiently strong—and they made no judgment about that, for we are all of us, each in our own special way, unique and individualistic!

We'll find something, NP promised, and they did. It happened that his soul's evolution, chartable through the generations, had prepared him exactly for this: to be a Listener. His fascination facility was undeveloped, naturally, but its potential was limitless. His receptivity, moreover, was near perfect, allowing him to encourage the transfer of pain, a faculty present in less than one percent of one percent of the population. Leonard could handle Neetsa Pizza complaints, in other words, so he did.

The White Room was a Neetsa Pizza innovation, the creation of which, under the off-site but highly supportive supervision of a Pythagorean Mentor, was an NP rite of passage. Over a three-day period (three because three dynamically bridges the dyadic gap between Listener and client-in-pain), Leonard had converted his grandfather's garage-apartment bedroom—dragging away the faded settee; painting the walls, onto which his grandfather had scrawled undisciplined columns of unreadable script; fastening flimsies to the windows and sixty-day sealant to the closets, all the while fasting and chanting the NP theme song. After the Whitening, his Mentor had wept with Leonard over the purity of the Room. Or rather, his Mentor had wept, while Leonard, in a dehydrated delirium, begged for food.

Books were forbidden in the White Room, as was any reading material other than the Pythagoras Papers and Listeners' Manual, as was Medusa, the neighborly cat. Needlework was off-limits, as were half-life pencils, solo-games, and other distractions. Between calls, Listeners were to memorize conversion scripts, play Listener problem-solving games, ruminate on the moral and aesthetic value of neat pizza, or practice a Company-developed form of meditation based on Pythagorean *echemythia*, or silence. Leonard had shown unusual *echemythia* aptitude but he found pretzeling hard on his knees, so with Felix's help he unfiltered his screen and installed true-ray blockers on his roof (his little rebellion) so NP couldn't overfly and see.

On night two, bereft of clients-in-pain, Leonard paced his White Room, again asking questions of the Brazen Head:

Q: Sue & Susheela—are they real? Are they married?

A: They exist. In this land, however, females cannot as yet marry each other. In a while, crocodile!

Leonard practiced his bonhomie, a skill that came less naturally to him than listening. Clients-in-pain with a justice record, he knew, find presumptions of familiarity deeply humiliating, while clients-in-pain from certain middling classes are comforted by probable nicknames, a preapproved list of which was offered by his screen, in ranked order of priority: Pher for Christopher, Don for Donna.

Good evening, Med! he said to Medusa the cat. How can I meet your Neetsa Pizza needs?

Top of the evening, Madame Medusa! Can I interest you in a Neetsa Pizza coupon?

Still he received no calls. No opportunities to relieve pain. By the third night, Leonard was frantic. His phone log showed the usual number of incomings, random call lengths within the expected range. When he tried calling one of those numbers he heard a soft static that somehow hurt his ears. What if Neetsa Pizza had achieved an optimal level of client satisfaction? This was everyone's dream, but what then? What other job would suit him half as well? He wasn't diminutive enough to be a barbecutie, and he was too polite to be a soda jerk. Caravan driver? Too much face-to-face. Water carrier? Leather beater? No screen time!

Panicked, Leonard reinstalled his screen filter, dismantled the true-ray blocker on his roof, and practiced Pythagorean silence with unprecedented focus.

The situation is dire, he told his sister, Carol, after his shift. He'd changed out of his white caftan and trousers into rainbow lounging shorts; she was getting ready for her day shift at Jack-o-Bites, where she served Scottish tapas in reprehensible tartan steep pants.

Carol was unsympathetic: You sedate the postindustrial masses with your pre-Socratic gobbledygook, she said, running a pick through her red afro. Pythagorean pizza is the opiate of the middle classes!

Is not! Leonard said.

Is too! she replied. Pass me my tam.

Carol only pretended to be a Jacobite: in fact, she was a neo-Maoist. According to her, the revolution would originate with suburbanites such as herself. It had to, for who was more oppressed, who more in need of radicalization? She took issue with Neetsa Pizza's rigid hierarchy, its notion that initiation was only for the lucky few—the oligarchy of it!

Pizza, she liked to exclaim, is nothing more than the ingredients that give it form.

No! Leonard would cry, shocked as ever by her materialism. There is such a thing as right proportion! Such a thing as beauty!

Leonard lacked his sister's sense that the world was broken. He'd been a coddled younger child, while she had been forced by the death of their parents to care for him and their doddering grandfather. No surprise she found the world in need of overhaul. In Leonard's view, bits of the world might be damaged, but never permanently so. It was his mission, through Listening, to heal some part of it. No need for reeducation, no need for armed struggle.

The Leader has assumed control of the menus, Carol said, pinning the tam to her afro. Did you even know? **FELIX, YOU BETTER BE PUTTING ON YOUR TOREADOR PANTS! YOUR CARAVAN LEAVES IN SEVEN MINUTES!** Pretty soon everyone will be selling Heraclitan Grillburgers, or whatever food he favors. You and I will both be out of a job.

(The food preferences of the Leader were, in the interests of National Unity, a well-kept secret.)

I didn't know, Leonard said, but he wasn't worried: Neetsa Pizza's concerns were eternal, not political: how to live the moral life, the unity underlying all manifestation. The Leader was undoubtedly aware of this.

You didn't know about the menus, did you? Carol said. I thought not. When was the last time you left the house?

I leave the house every day, as you well know, Leonard said— for at 3:23 p.m. each day Leonard walked to the corner of Boise and Degas to pick up Felix, whom he cared for after school in exchange for living rent-free in Carol's garage apartment, without which he would have been Out in the World Alone.

7

I don't mean the corner, Carol said.

I don't need to leave the house, Leonard said, and he didn't. He was perfectly fulfilled in his White Room, and joyous in his Life Plan, which was to heal clients-in-pain. It was a good life, its pieces fitting together like the double crust on Carol's Chicken-in-Every-Pot Pie.

You need to leave the house, Carol said, fastening her tartan apron around her pleated steep pants. End of discussion. **FELIX!**

A breathless boy arrived, bedecked in black-trimmed red toreador pants and holding a junior clutchbag. His red afro was disheveled and he looked vaguely worried. This was Felix.

Go, Carol said. Don't believe a word your teachers tell you.

Three twenty-three, Leonard said.

Felix nodded all-purposefully, then ran to catch his caravan.

A good egg

After Carol left, Leonard helped himself to haggis tarts, smuggled (as a form of revolutionary sabotage) by his sister from Jack-o-Bites. He checked that his White Room was perfectly white, then fretted about his missing complaints, Medusa on his lap.

He fell asleep on his swirly chair and dreamed of his grandfather. The old man smelled of herring and was holding an improbably tall stack of leather-bound books.

Boychik, the old man said. You're a good egg. I need you to listen good.

No problem, Leonard said. I'm a Listener. What's it like being dead?

You're not listening, his grandfather said. I need you to listen good.

Oh, Leonard said. I miss you. There was something I needed to tell you, I forget what.

It is time for you to save the world, his grandfather said. I need you to do this one thing for me. Boychik, are you listening?

Gosh, I'm glad to see you! Leonard said.

The world, boychik! You need to save the world!

Are you holding my calls, Grandfather? Somebody's holding my calls. I'm worried I'll lose my job—then what'll I do?

But that wasn't what he'd wanted to say. It was important, whatever it was.

Calls, shmalls! his grandfather said. I need you to listen!

Leonard remembered what it was.

I'm sorry, he said, extending his hand, but his grandfather was gone.

His family obligations

That afternoon, still thinking about his dream, Leonard brought a cup of chicory to the corner. Felix was too old by half to be met *at* the caravan, but he liked seeing Leonard half a block away—looking off, as if arrested by a compelling thought, his green army pants suavely sweeping the ground, his brown afro shining in the sunlight. On his way to the corner, however, Leonard was stopped by six policemen carrying sniper muskets and wearing yellow sashes that read **CHIPMUNK PATROL**.

Chipmunk Patrol?

They asked if Leonard was skulking, reminded him that the

webcam was always watching, offered him a pamphlet of inspiring homilies by the Leader.

He took two. No, better yet, three! As one, the Chipmunk Patrol squinted meaningfully, then walked away, looking at Leonard again over their collective shoulders.

The caravan arrived, discharging Felix. No black eye this time, but his toreador pants had been soiled. The municipal compost heap: it happened nearly every day.

Between the corner and home—territory officially known as the Time between Here and There—Felix was required to tell Leonard anything not-good that happened at school. So he wouldn't have to bring it home. On this day, head hanging low, Felix merely said, Do you think they're salvageable? Meaning his pants.

I have a surprise for you, Leonard said.

Is it . . . ?

You'll see, Leonard said. Already the boy's face had brightened.

Shall we run? Felix asked.

We shall! Leonard said.

The letters are dancing

Once home, Leonard put Felix's toreador pants into the steam-cleaner, then gave him ginger ale in a chilled beer stein and precisely two peanut-butter jam squares. Then he supervised five minutes of awesome karate kicks, after which Felix pronounced himself knackered and ready for a story.

Leonard wasn't good at stories. In the early days, when

Felix clambered onto his lap, Leonard would say, Once upon a time . . . , and Felix would say, What? What? and Leonard would say, There lived . . . , and Felix would say, Who? Who? thus creating an artificial suspense that ultimately proved unsatisfying. What Leonard quickly learned was that Felix was very good at stories, so much so that all Leonard had to say was, Who should our story be about today? and Felix would say, A beautiful princess named Celeste! and Leonard would say, Oh, and where does Celeste live? and Felix would say, In a great wooded land surrounded by beasties! and Leonard would say, Beasties, oh my! and Felix, his pale cheeks pinkening, would say, They're horrible! They dump boys onto the municipal compost heap! and on it would go.

After storytelling, if Felix wasn't too knackered, he would work on his opus, a finely drawn comic-book retelling of "Leonard's" stories. He was patient and careful, finishing no more than three or four panels per day, his retelling of the story always an improvement on the telling itself.

Don't you want your surprise? Leonard asked after the awesome karate kicks.

The White Room! Felix had forgotten!

Every sixty days, the seal to Grandfather's closet popped open and Leonard allowed Felix into the White Room. Felix put on a white overshirt and either his white toreador pants or white Laplander shorts, depending on the weather. Once in the Room, the boy would say a charm of his own devising, then close his eyes and pick a book at random. Then he'd sit on Leonard's lap and balance the book on their four knees. Leonard had no use for books—they reminded him of school, which he left at fifteen after learning about little other than the life of the Leader, and hygiene, both physical and social. He'd even less use for his grandfather's morocco-bound books, which were heavy and written in a language Leonard couldn't understand. Felix, however, seemed to have a feel for them.

Most of the books they "read" contained a central text in Hebrew, surrounded by columns also in Hebrew but in a smaller hand.

Not Hebrew, Felix said. Aramaic. It's called the Talmud, which is actually a lot of books. I asked the Brazen Head.

Felix was always asking things of the Brazen Head. Like Leonard, Felix enjoyed his screen time, when his mother allowed it. When Carol told him to go outside and play, he swung halfheartedly on a creaky safety swing till he was allowed back in. When he was younger she used to organize play dates with proletariat children, but in their vigorous class-based outrage they, like his middle-class chums, were often moved to throw Felix onto the municipal compost heap. Peasant children were no better. Carol reckoned she didn't have time for all that laundry.

Sure you're not provoking them? she'd asked.

They say carrot tops belong with carrot tops.

And what do you say to that?

Mom!

Alright! Alright!

So it was that Felix had more screen time than was good for a revolutionary boy and could ask questions of the Brazen Head. He especially liked giving the Head fantastic instructions: Use mutant robot zombies to collect the infofiles! Use color-coded carrier pigeons! Bake the answers in a jujuberry pie! The Brazen Head would signal his disdain for such fancy by sitting on the color-coded pigeons until answers oozed from under his buttocks and trickled down the legs of his gilded throne.

Because neither uncle nor nephew could read Hebrew, or

Aramaic, they usually told each other stories about what Grandfather's book probably said. Usually this meant stories about a beautiful princess named Celeste.

Except on this day. On this day, Felix chose a book not much bigger than his hand, with silver cornerpieces and a complex pattern stamped on its leather binding. Instead of starting a story, Felix stared at the yellow pages, which seemed impossibly thin, and said, I think I need glasses. Can you see? Leonard, can you see? The letters are dancing.

He's better than us

Felix insisted he could "read" the dancing letters. *Gate of Reincarnations*, he said. What's that?

Where could Felix have gotten that word? Leonard doubted very much that it was part of Felix's Integrative Optimal-Learning Curriculum.

Well, Leonard said, Pythagoras believed that after we die, our souls are reborn in new bodies. He called it metempsychosis or transmigration; that's basically the same as reincarnation.

Why is the soul reborn? Felix asked. I thought it went to heaven, where it was eaten by worms and happily tilled by peasant women and men.

Different people think different things, I guess. Pythagoras believed that we reincarnate so we can perfect our souls.

Like ... like Grandfather might be reborn? As a cat, you mean? Felix asked.

Medusa meowed; Leonard hadn't realized she was in the room, but there she was, a coil of shiny fur by their feet.

I guess, Leonard said. So what does the story say? And he listened as Felix "read" about a guy named Chaim, who had apparently given a lot of thought to reincarnation. Leonard found Felix's performance charming, if somewhat disturbing.

Is Celeste in this story? Leonard asked.

No, Felix said. But listen, and he explained how there are gilguls (I'm sorry, he said, I can't come up with a better word for it) who enter a body at birth and stay with that body its whole lifetime.

What about the municipal compost heap? Leonard asked. Is that in the story? Or beasties?

No, Felix said. Listen, and he explained how there are two types of ibbur, which are reincarnations on purpose: when a righteous soul enters a grown body either to perfect itself or to help the soul of that body become more righteous.

That's good to know, Leonard said, and said no more as Felix traced the many incarnations of Mr. Chaim, whose name, Felix explained, means life.

When Carol returned, Leonard didn't worry her about soiled toreador pants or Felix's hallucinations or perplexing tales; he noted only that the boy might be weary. A nap, he suggested, or time off from school?

Felix has to go to school, Carol said, pulling cold bannocks and Scotch pies from a secret compartment in her silver travel vest. He has to understand the enemy if he's to lead the revolution.

Like many mothers, Carol had big plans for her son.

If the police come to the door, pretend you're sleeping, she said, finding an air-resistant container for the bannocks and pies.

Why would the police come to the door?

They wouldn't. Just as a general rule, a precept to live by.

Oh, Leonard said. Have you seen this new Chipmunk Patrol?

If they stop you with Felix, pretend you don't know me.

Are you in trouble? Leonard asked.

Why would I be in trouble? All I do is sling bannocks, take care of you guys, and spend time with my book club.

I have to go to work, Leonard said.

I can see that, she said, looking pointedly at his all-white vestments. He'd taken special care with them that evening, perfuming his caftan and pressing his trousers into seven sharp pleats.

You need to be careful with Felix, Carol said. He's better than us, you know.

I know, Leonard said.

Messer Marco

Leonard approached his White Room with special reverence. He could not imagine working for any other chain. NP was committed to supporting its Listeners in every possible way—through innovative aptitude testing, exhaustive training, thoughtful supply of easy-to-use Pythagorean materials, provision of periodic "refresher" updates. The sole support Carol got from Jack-o-Bites was laundry service for her tartan steep pants. He'd heard from screen-yakking Listeners that all the Heraclitan flame-throwers got was a can of Flame-Off, should they set fire to their limbs.

Leonard repaid NP's faith by working hard. He memorized

conversion scripts for all known and anticipated Scenarios: wrong numbers, solicitations, pollsters, obscene callers, lonely widowers, cranks asking for itsy-bitsy Neetsa Pizzas, smart-alecks wanting to know how a company that preached trans-migration could sell robin's egg pizza, and so on. Eighty-six percent of Leonard's complaint calls and seventeen percent of his "off" calls converted—which is to say, the caller accepted and redeemed a Neetsa Pizza coupon—by far a company record, but low, considering Leonard's Special Gift.

Fulfillment of Leonard's Special Gift was limited by two factors. First, an almost antisocial unwillingness to obey all rules exactly to the letter (hence the true-ray blocker on the roof); second, a tendency to display less than Total Compassion when mocked. When a crank called, Leonard would make one, possibly two scripted conversion attempts, but if the crank persisted, he would, very much against Neetsa Pizza policy, terminate the session.

This would change! Given another chance, Leonard would show optimal compassion in every possible Scenario!

Before even opening the door to his White Room, he engaged in a five-minute Pythagorean meditation, ignoring Medusa, who twirled about his legs. He then swept the inside clean again, lest the Room's purity be compromised by even one speck of dust. Then he retrieved his Pythagoras Papers from their specially molded slot by the screen.

He hadn't read his Papers since Basic Training, though his NP vow obligated him to do so every day. He sat on his swirly chair within reach of the phone and pondered cartoons illustrating those concepts he'd found most interesting in boot camp—eternal recurrence, for example, which holds that everything that happens now has happened before—which Leonard found rather disturbing. Did it mean that someone like him had already sat in a White Room fretting about missing complaints? What did that Leonard do about it? Weren't White Rooms a new phenomenon, one of six Neetsa Pizza innovations for the new millennium (six being Pythagoras's first perfect number, the sum of its aliquot parts: 1+2+3)? Did it mean merely that someone like (or unlike) Leonard had waited somewhere for something that was missing and important? If that were the case, the concept didn't mean much, did it?

When he added metempsychosis, or reincarnation, to the mix, his head began to hurt. Is it the same reincarnated soul who sits in the White Room over and over again waiting for complaints, and isn't that rather like hell, to experience the same life over and over again? What was the point? Does the reincarnated soul remember its past? If so, maybe that soul learned what to do about the missing whatevers—but then he wouldn't experience those same things over and over again, would he? Or did the same incidents rotate to different souls so that everyone got to experience everything at one time or another, in which case that might be interesting. But what if the soul reincarnated as a grasshopper? Did grasshoppers experience the grasshopper equivalent of waiting for missing calls in a White Room?

Did Mr. Chaim have an answer for these weighty questions? Leonard wondered, and then the phone rang—or rather, it bleated feebly, like a sick lamb.

Leonard's training kicked in. He took a deep breath, centered himself in his body, and allowed compassion to well in his probably reincarnated though not necessarily any-the-wiser soul.

Neetsa Pizza, we make it neat, he said. How can I meet your Neetsa Pizza needs?

Isaac? a male voice said. I have been dreaming of you. You are blind, are you not?

A crank. Of course. But for once, Leonard didn't care. He referred to his screen for guidance. There he would find caller name, country of origin, previous history of pain, photo, justice record, ideological patterns (as represented by previous fast-food choices), and socioeconomic indicators, all routed through preapproved Listener algorithms, generating an optimal client-satisfaction strategy, as well as helpful tips, hints, pointers, and clues.

Only it didn't. Caller information instead spun about his screen, a caroming jumble of letters and numbers. Without his optimal client-satisfaction strategy, Leonard would have to wing it, something he didn't much like doing.

Neetsa Pizza, he said. Have you tried our mouthwatering isosceles sage pizza, loved by wise men the world over? What about our heavenly spherical pizza . . .

Pizza? the man asked. What's that?

Leonard hung up.

The man called back.

You are Isaac, perhaps? I see your caftan in my dreams. It tells me you are of the Hebrew faith, resident of the Languedoc region. Dead some fifty years, if I am not mistaken. What can I do for you, Messer Isaac?

A man with an accent. A mentally deficient man with a very strong accent (rather like an accent on an accent). A Client Very Much Not Like Me! This could be a Neetsa Pizza test, Leonard realized. His Mentor had told him about such things.

This is Leonard, he answered, taking special care with his enunciation. How can I meet your Neetsa Pizza needs?

You are not Isaac?

This is Leonard, Leonard said, pleased that he had made himself understood and sensing conversion opportunity in the man's hesitation. What is your name, good sir?

My Christian name is Marco, but friends call me Milione.

Where are you, Mill? May I send you a pizza coupon?

I am in prison, as the whole world knows. What is a coupon?

Leonard hung up.

The man called back.

Don't you have someone else to call? Leonard asked.

I have the feeling I am meant to communicate with someone named Isaac. Is he there?

Maybe you should check the number.

Number?

Click.

Mill called several times, always surprised to find Leonard. He was imprisoned in Genova, he said, which Leonard was fairly sure was in the Finger Lakes District.

Am I speaking with Messer Isaac? the man invariably asked.

It's me, Leonard, like last time. Don't you have something better to do?

Alas, no. I am in prison.

And innocent, of course—a man of stature and achievement, guilty of nothing more than love of country. For which "crime" he was forced to share a cell with braggarts and brigands. Did Leonard, perhaps, hold sway with the duke?

He did not.

Of one thing Leonard was certain: this man was not, as he said, a prisoner of war. More likely, a loco in a loony bin. With a phone scrambler that haywired Leonard's screen.

Understanding this, Leonard allowed compassion to surge and well.

I would like to help you, he said. Tell me how I can help you.

Who are you, esteemed friend? Mill asked. Whom have I reached on this mystical journey, if you are not to be my deliverer?

We don't deliver to prison, Leonard said.

You are sure you are not Isaac?

I am Leonard, of Neetsa Pizza? We talked earlier.

Leonardo of Pisa? Prince Leonardo of Pisa? Why didn't you say this? Your Grace, I have a message for your sister.

I am just Leonard. Would you like a coupon for our uniquely delicious "thick and thin" pizza, optimally designed for loved ones who stick by you? he suggested, congratulating himself on his innovative use of the Lateral Sales Strategy.

Loved ones? You mean my father and uncle? What use have they for gifts! They got the lion's share of the jewels, don't forget! Mill chuckled. I am well into my fifth decade, Messer Leonardo, but still they call me little Marco, tiny Marco, eensy-weensy Marco. Have you relatives such as these?

Leonard, please. A sister, Carol. She's older. And a grand-father, but he passed. And a nephew, Felix. I am an orphan, he added, remembering that the strategic sharing of Personal Information can create empathy bonds with callers in their fifth decade.

I too! Mill said. An orphan until the age of fifteen. Which is when my father returned. Can you imagine my astonishment? The auntie who raised me told me he was dead!

That must have made you very happy, Leonard essayed. (He would have been happy to see his father again at any age.)

My auntie taught me penmanship and Bible verses, she wanted me for the Church, but I yearned for manly things. To join my father on those dread seas, to discover new lands! I yearned for adventure! My father, seeing that I was no longer a suckling babe, claimed me for his own and brought me to Acre. Have you been to Cathay?

I don't think so, said Leonard.

You'd know if you had. Other places of interest? The Levant, perhaps?

I haven't traveled, Leonard said. I'm only twenty-four.

Mill exploded in mirth; his laugh was low and wheezy.

By your age, good sir, I had crossed the whole flat earth! Find yourself a ship! Nothing compares with exploration: it enlivens the senses and broadens the mind—and the women! You have never seen such women!

Women? Leonard asked, despite himself.

Women! Mill said.

Tell me, Leonard said in a small voice.

Ah, the women! Mill said, evidently remembering the women.

Please? Leonard said.

You could never imagine there were so many types of women, Mill said. Truly! Brown women—did you know there were brown women?

Never mind, Leonard said.

The women of Tun and Kain, near the Solitary Tree—now, they are lovely, Mill said. The girls of Muhelet are perhaps the world's most beautiful; but the women of Kinsai—ah, the women of Kinsai!

It's okay, Leonard said. I don't need to hear any more.

The Golden King of Caichu is attended only by damsels—can you imagine? Damsels pull his chariot! The world is full of wonders, Leonardo; you must investigate!

I am not so good with women, Leonard said.

Not a problem! In the province of Kamul, men lend their wives to passing travelers. No need for pretty words: they go willingly! This is the practice in Kaindu as well, near the turquoise mountain. Now, in Tibet . . .

The line went dead.

Mill called back. In Tibet, he said, and again the phone went dead.

In a certain province the name of which I may not mention, he said when he called back, no honorable man may marry a virgin! To prove she is favored by the gods, she must dally with as many men as possible—only then may she marry. A perfect place for a quiet man like you. If that does not suit, there are twenty thousand women of the world living in the suburbs of Khan-balik; the Great Khan makes them available to all ambassadors. We could go there together—you as ambassador from the great land of Pisa, I representing my native Venice! I have seen a land, he whispered, where women of quality wear trousers.

Can we change the subject? Leonard asked.

It is exactly as I say! Mill said.

I'm kind of stuck here, Leonard said. I can't go anywhere.

I apologize, dear friend. Perhaps you also are in prison?

Feels like it sometimes.

Oh, dear! What had Leonard said? If NP were testing his skills with Clients Very Much Not Like Me, they didn't need to know that the White Room sometimes felt like a prison. They wouldn't understand that Leonard liked it that way.

I am most sorry, Mill said gravely. Who shares your cell, if I may inquire?

You mean, do I have a group plan? Are you selling minutes?

(Leonard's Brazen Head satellite-cell minutes came from Neetsa Pizza, but if he were to lose his job???)

What a quaint idea! Would that I could sell minutes, for I sense that time is running short. Forgive the poor translation: I am, as yet, inexpert in this form of communication. I am wondering what manner of man shares your temporary dungeon habitat.

Leonard explained that he lived and worked alone; Mill couldn't believe it.

This must be the greatest torment of all: to be always alone!

I like it, Leonard said. And he did: solving problems with a pizza coupon was as much people as Leonard generally wanted.

I, on the other hand, Mill said, am surrounded by prisoners of the lowest class! Riffraff, ruffians, and bowlegged bastards!

My! Leonard said.

And visitors. Mill had been in his "temporary dungeon habitat" less than one week, but already news of his incarceration had reached the noblest society. Fine ladies visited him, eager to hear his tales. Some brought sweetmeats or news from home, the prettiest promised him things with their eyes, all assured him they'd do what they could.

I'm sure they will, Leonard said, aware that he'd all but given up on conversion.

Humph, said Mill. Tell me about your temporary dungeon habitat. Is it dank, does water drip down the rough-hewn stone?

Actually, it's white. Everything is white. I paint it every year.

No past inmate has scratched poems on the mortar?

Leonard laughed, then remembered the strange, unreadable scrawls his grandfather had left on his walls, before the room became White. His grandfather had asked, each year on Leonard's birthday, whether Leonard could read what he'd written there; each year Leonard was not up to the task.

No poems, he said.

Do you have a window? Mill persisted. Can you hear the children playing?

It's night. The children are all in bed.

Night? Mill said. My good friend, it's well past dawn.

I do the midnight shift, Leonard said. It's definitely night.

I implore you, do not let your mind slip! I am looking out the window and plainly it is day: ships are active, gulls fly, wenches lift their skirts for sailors.

Sometimes you have to let a client have the last word.

If it were day and I could see out the window, Leonard said, I'd see buildings just like this one.

What a benighted land! Mill murmured. So many prisons! We face the port, of course. This is how my captors torment me! I thought I saw Uncle Maffeo on a boat much like the one the Great Khan gave us to escort the Princess Kokachin to Arghun of the Levant.

Mill was silent a moment.

It was just a vision, Mill concluded in a sad voice, of the sort I have frequently had since crossing the Desert of Lop. You've met them, I assume? The Tibetans?

The line went dead.

Prison and the White Room

Over the next few nights, Mill was Leonard's only caller. Leonard grew accustomed to the phone's gentle bleating and Mill's jovial but strangely distant, overly accented voice. Reassured that this was not an NP test, Leonard reinstalled his true-ray blocker, unfiltered his screen, and left bannocks by the cat-chimney.

How long have you been in your temporary dungeon habitat? Mill asked. Perhaps you too have just arrived?

Three years.

My friend! How is it that you have not gone mad! Have you a beard down to your belly? I am glad to have found you—do not despair! I shall relate stories to you, wonders such as you have never known! The days will fly!

Okay, Leonard said.

And so he began. Mostly Mill's tales were not so wondrous. He had much to say about the availability in dull-sounding countries of water, food, and game. He spoke of climate and wind and pasturage for beasts. Of cloth and carpets and dates. Of deserts and steeds and falcons and asses. Leonard couldn't share Mill's enthusiasm for the particulars of what he called Custom and Commerce. He also couldn't follow Mill's specious geography, for he could find no Lesser Armenia on the map he'd printed and illegally affixed to his white wall, no Persia, no Levant—certainly no Desert of Lop! But still Leonard listened, because compassion welled, and because his screen hissed whenever he turned it on, and because occasionally Mill described something of interest, like mountains of salt, or a lake that produced fish only during Lent (whatever that was), or a caliph who starved to death in a tower of gold. A shoemaker who gouged out his eye because he had taken too great a pleasure in one lady's foot. Date wine that loosened the bowels, three kings who threw a magic stone into a well, a hot wind that stifled armies, professional mourners who never ceased lamenting.

Adventures too: Mill was pursued once by a renegade khan, narrowly escaping capture; many of his companions were not so lucky. He spoke of fierce Saracens, of whom any evil might be expected; also, marauding Tartars and his friends, the Tibetans.

Tell me, Mill said, once he'd called back, does this not sound like the life for you? Every night a new bed, every day something you never imagined?

No! Leonard said. How do you stand it? Don't new things frighten you? Wouldn't you rather be safe at home?

I have no home! My home is where I am, wherever that may be. That is freedom, that is happiness!

Leonard pondered the world outside his White Room, outside his sister's house, beyond the corners of Boise and Degas. His stomach became distinctly unsettled.

I think you're very brave, Leonard said.

What you call bravery is easier than the alternative.

Which is?

Fear. And isolation from one's fellows. But truly, one is brave only if one pursues what one fears, and I do not fear the unknown.

What do you fear? Leonard asked.

. . .

Mill? Leonard asked.

I suppose this place, Mill said softly. The sameness of it, the smallness. It does not resemble the desert I have mentioned, yet it shares many of its qualities; at night I tremble, much as I trembled there, before I met them. It is the emptiness I fear, emptiness and being alone. Here is where I must be brave.

Oh, Leonard said.

But all places have their fascination, even this one—you will learn this once you leave your temporary dungeon habitat, as soon you shall, I am sure. You have only to pay attention, to give yourself over to wonder. On this very subject, tell me, what do merchants trade in your land?

Leonard had to think a moment.

I have no religion, Leonard said.

Silence.

You are a Saracen, then? You worship Mahomet?

I don't believe in God, Leonard said.

Again, silence.

You are a Tartar, then? An idolater? A fire worshipper?

I have no religion, Leonard said. I worship nothing.

A silence so long, Leonard thought the line had gone dead.

I have seen many wonders, my friend, but none so strange as this. In Fu-chau, I met persons who were Christian and did not know it! I had to explain this most important fact to them! Papa insists they were Manichean. Whatever the case, at least they held some belief.

My family's Jewish, if that helps, Leonard said. My grandfather's grandfather was a rabbi.

Ah! You have been excommunicated. I am very sorry. I am a member of the true faith, of course, a devoted subject of Pope Boniface VIII.

Pope what?

You do not know Boniface? He is no more?

Leonard was astonished to hear Mill weep, and again allowed compassion to well. But then Mill said, It seems only yesterday Gregory named us official legates to the Great Khan—and Leonard didn't feel so bad.

And so it went: Mill calling several times a night, Leonard eventually communicating the concept of call queuing so he could excuse himself should a real call come through, which it did not. His phone logs continued to fill, he seemed even to be increasing his conversion rate, for which accomplishment NP sent him a semiprecious, metal-plated, equilateral calzone.

Leonard didn't mind talking with Mill, especially now that

his screen was acting so strange, with Sue & Susheela
most of the time, the Brazen Head too (a note—*Out*
taped to its head). When Mill called, those sites dissolv
tallizing into diamonds scattered brilliant at the bottor
screen—touching one, Leonard got an electric shock.
minutes after Mill's calls, his sites would crawl back, e
and ill formed. Sue & Susheela would be grumpy, the
Head would blink stupidly and belch.

Leonard still hung up on Mill from time to time. W
called back, as always he would, he didn't seem both
fact, he blamed himself.

Forgive me, he'd say. I learned much from the Tibe
I am no adept.

Then, invariably, the line would go dead.

Four men walk into an orchard

Six men with justice sticks came to Carol's house—the
their police caravans should have awakened Leonard,
not. Carol made Felix answer the door.

My mother is out planting flowers in honor of th
Felix said. Would you like some claggum?

They took their treacle treats with them, and Carol
clutchbag crammed with papers into the fire.

Records from my book group, she explained. Or so
during his Time between Here and There. Which w
longer every day. There was more and more Felix coul
home—not just unkind classmates and ungraspable n
ical concepts, but hard-to-put-a-finger-on fears. To get

I know that story, Leonard said, stunned.

You do?

I do, Leonard said. But he didn't have a chance to remember how because Felix was crying.

I'm scared, he said. What do you think they saw?

The clapping song

Carol was making revolutionary stew in her all-around cooker when Leonard finished work the next morning and wandered into the stoveroom for chicory. There was nothing truly revolutionary about Carol's stew except that (1) the ingredients remind us of our agrarian past, wherein lie the ancient roots of revolution; (2) all flavors have their say in a stew, as they must in any socialist system; and (3) like history, it takes a long time to cook but it's worth it in the end.

Felix is worried, Leonard said.

About what?

This and that. Men with justice sticks coming to the door.

I don't know what you're talking about.

Carol had finished chopping the vegetables and was hacking at a clump of meat with a cleaver.

You don't know what I'm talking about?

Felix has a vivid imagination. You shouldn't encourage him [*thwack!*].

I just listen, Leonard said.

You don't just listen—you tell him stories, and you encourage that comic-book opus of his.

Speaking of stories, did Grandpa tell you any? Leonard asked, plucking a revolutionary carrot from the pot.

Of course he didn't [*thwack!*]. Stories were for the grandson, remember? You were the all-important grandson, I was the not-at-all-important granddaughter [*thwack!*].

Maybe a story about an orchard? I sort of remembered it the other day, he said, unwilling to explain that Felix had dreamt it, more or less in its entirety. And bits of others, but they're all jumbled. He made me promise to tell them to my grandson, but if I don't remember them, how can I do that?

You'll never have grandsons if you don't leave the house [*thwack!*].

Sure you don't remember any?

Carol put down her cleaver. I may have possibly heard something through the door.

Yeah?

Like a song?

A song?

A clapping song?

Oh, Leonard said. Sing it to me. Please?

He used to make you sing it to him every day. Do you really not remember?

I don't. Can you sing it? Please?

You can't teach this shite to my son, Carol said.

Please?

And so Carol did:

Who is the king of the [*clap*] third ether?
Trick question!
There are [clap] *three parts to the* [clap] *third ether!*

Asmodeus is the king of the [clap] upper ether! And Lesser Lilith is his wife!

By this point, Leonard was able to join Carol in the singing, and more: he performed the dance that went with it; it wasn't something he could control.

Kafkaphony is the king of the [clap] middle ether! And Kafkaphony has two wives!
Sarita is his wife for the [clap] first six months! Sagrirta is his wife for the second!
Kafsephony is the king of the [clap] bottom ether! And Mehetzabel is his wife!
Who is the king of [clap] all the demons?
Samael is the king of [clap] all the demons! And great Lilith is his wife!
Oh, yes, Samael is the king of [clap] all the demons. Samael is king of them all!

That man was a lunatic, Carol said, returning to her meat. I should never have let you near him.

The singing and dancing left Leonard shaky. It was as if they'd opened a hole in the universe, and through it poured everything he had felt when his grandfather died—sorrow, and loneliness dry as a desert, and regret for the things he'd said during his grandfather's last days. And memories—of the old man's old-man smell, the chewing tobacco that stuck in his beard, the incomprehensible jokes he told about herring—and with them, all the stories his grandfather had ever told him, whole.

Mountains of salt

For several nights, Mill continued to describe his unfollowable itinerary from west to east, though his enthusiasm began to wane on the road to Cathay. Where he used to delight in describing corn markets and boiled wine, he now omitted detail and spoke as if by rote.

When Leonard inquired, Mill said he'd lost some of his native optimism. Lords and ladies continued to crowd his cell. They clamored for stories of his adventures, but Mill now found them irksome. Tell us about men with tails, they begged, tell us about men with earrings! Did you meet Prester John? Was the khan very manly? Is it true he had six dozen wives, some of them Carmelite nuns?

Those fops and coquettes didn't share Mill's fascination with Custom and Commerce—imagine! They brought their friends, they whispered and pointed as if Mill were a unicorn or porcupine. He no longer believed their promises: how would they amuse themselves if he were free?

In the evenings, he found himself alone with his fellows; they despised him for his special treatment, the obligation they felt when his guests arrived to remove their ragged, stinking selves to the edges of the cell. It was only because he shared his spoils, his cheeses and dried meats, that they didn't violate him at night. He slept little in any case, for the sounds of their shitting, their resentful snores and creaks and cries, were louder and more noisome than anything he'd experienced at sea.

So Mill sighed and fell into deep silences, sometimes in the middle of a story. Leonard had to use all of his Listening skills to keep Mill going. He might hear Mill speak of the smell of the sea mingling with that of my saltwater tears and say, Where were we? You were describing the idolaters who buy beautiful wives . . .

The fat idolaters with small noses? Mill would ask.

Those exactly! Leonard would exclaim.

Yes, Mill would say, and he'd continue awhile longer, speaking without passion about dried melons, bandits, and lions; horned horses descended from Bucephalus. Idolaters who change the weather and cause statues to speak. Plains, mountains, and gorges; orchards, vineyards, and jeweled mountains; kings, counts, and khans.

Interesting! Leonard would say, and it was, mostly, compared with his White Room, which seemed whiter to him now, and more quiet than ever.

Really? Mill asked. I find none of it so interesting these days as that ship out there, or that bird flying up above.

You'll be out soon, Leonard said, but he was doubtful—and in fact, he wasn't sure Mill should be released. What would he do out in the world? Become one of those dirty men who travel in packs, stealing food from municipal compost heaps and begging at NP security windows? If he became troublesome they might brand him and force him outside the city walls. Mill might be crazy, but he didn't deserve that.

Yes, my friend, Mill said, I will be outside soon—as will you, I am sure. But to what end? I have taken that desert, the name of which I dare not speak, inside me. I am sere, do you understand?

Maybe, Leonard said. I think so.

I fear I shall ever be. In prison or without, it shall always be the same. I am become the desert, dear Leonard.

Lonely, Leonard said.

Yes, Mill replied.

And lost, Leonard said. No Hello! lamps on Everything's-Okay poles to show the way.

What a way you have with words! Mill replied. Oh, I long for the consolation of a woman! Do you ever feel this way?

Sometimes, Leonard said. Well, yes, all the time.

This shall be my first task after I am released: to find a wife. Have you a wife, dear Leonard? Perhaps some suckling babes?

I am only twenty-four, Leonard reminded him.

It is not too late! Mill said. Have you ever been with a European woman? A free European woman?

No, Leonard had to confess.

I neither, Mill said, and sighed. Just port prostitutes and slaves, and the women I spoke of earlier. Why did you never marry?

I am not so good with women, Leonard said.

Yes, yes, you have said this. But what skill do you lack? I am told that women are simple: they care only for wealth, position, and pretty compliments.

I'll remember that, Leonard said, miserable.

Except Kokachin, Mill said thoughtfully. Kokachin was different.

Different?

She cared only that I listen.

I can do that! Leonard said. I can listen!

Hers was not a happy life, Mill added.

No?

I must go, Mill said, his voice shaking.

Time for bannocks

When Leonard went down to the house after his shift, he was surprised not to find Carol. She should have been flattening steep pants or making nourishment for Felix. He checked the stoveroom, the gameroom, Carol's room. Though the latter was in its customary state of tumbled chaos—no knowing whether she'd slept there that night, or was there still, under a pile of crumpled leisure garb. He poked at the pile. She was not there.

He found Felix standing by the window in his bedroom, still wearing his ivy-green sleeping togs.

Where's your mother? he asked, putting his arm on the boy's shoulder.

I don't know, Felix said. She didn't come back from her book group.

You've been waiting all night?

I was worried.

You should have come to me.

I didn't want you to worry.

It's my job to worry, I'm a grown-up.

You are?

Of course I am.

Probably she was out with her book club and missed curfew, Felix said.

Probably, Leonard said. Did you sleep at all?

Not so much, Felix said.

Have you moved from the window since she left?

Not really, Felix said.

It was dark, you couldn't see anything, Leonard said.

I could see, said Felix.

Stay home today, said Leonard. That way when your mother gets back, you'll know she's safe. And you can nap.

With Medusa?

If she's willing. It's hard to tell a cat what to do.

I tell her what to do.

She does what you say?

Unless I tell her to do something like fly, then she just gives me a look.

Time for bannocks, Leonard said.

What are you doing in my house?

When Carol finally returned it was several hours past dawn. Felix was sleeping in his room with Medusa, whom Leonard had lured into the house with haggis. Leonard was sitting in Felix's swirly chair, ready for sleep himself, but he'd promised to stay awake so Felix wouldn't have to.

He heard Carol's tiptoeing; she herself, with her whisper-quiet sailing shoes, was silent but her house had a problem with creaking, especially in the morning. Leonard tiptoed out to meet her. She was wearing her black climbing suit and dust cap, but her face was sooted black and she smelled like ... burnt hair?

Carol?

What are you doing in my house?

Carol? Are you okay?

Why aren't you sleeping? You're supposed to be in your garage sleeping!

Felix is sleeping; I'm waiting for you—he was worried.

Felix is sleeping? He's supposed to be at school!

Shh! You'll wake him! Have you been ... burning things?

If Felix doesn't go to school, people ask questions!

Leonard tried to allow compassion to well so he could listen, but he was angry.

You have no right! he said. You have no right to put Felix in danger!

I may not have the right to do what's right in this country, but I do have the obligation.

I don't understand.

You're a child, Leonard. You're as much a child as you ever were. I'm sure that's my fault somehow. Out of my way. I need to change for work.

How will you explain being late?

I won't have to. Certain of our caravans are ... dysfunctioning. Food workers all over town will be late today. Now move, she said, and pushed past.

Carol? Are you bleeding? Carol?

Cathay noodles

You are my only friend, Mill exclaimed that night. My truest and only friend! You will not forsake me, will you? Speaking to you through this mystical connection—it is saving me, I assure you.

You must have other friends, Leonard said. What about from your travels?

For a moment Mill didn't reply.

So many have been lost. You have no idea. On the journey back to the Levant, we lost all but eighteen—nearly six hundred souls, gone! Everyone who went with me into the desert ... I came home then to nothing. My father came back all those years ago to a son he'd quite forgotten, my uncle was glad to see his wife, but on my return what had I, other than triumph and my past? No wife, no children, no land. A small voice suggested I command a galley, so I agreed: better to fight a war than be still and alone, and look where it led me: to this place where there is aught to do but think about the past!

To distract Mill from his melancholy, Leonard asked whether there were friendly folk among the ruffians in his cell.

A monk arrived yesterday, Mill whispered. He took exception to his friary's midday meal and set the refectory alight. Imagine his reaction when he sees the swill we must eat! I'd sooner dine on Pharoah's rats and Tartar milk paste! What do they feed you, dear Leonard?

Neetsa pizza, Leonard said, though he'd quite given up hope for conversion. Golden Mean is my favorite: pepperoni and cheese in perfect proportion.

You speak in riddles, my friend. One reason I enjoy our conversation!

What would you eat if you could have anything delivered to your cell?

Cathay noodles! Mill said. Oh, how I long for Cathay noodles.

Then he fell into madness, as so often he did, his voice dropping:

Dear Leonard, please forget I mentioned Cathay noodles. I have quite lost my head. Tell no one I spoke of them! No one must know about the noodles!

Okay, Leonard said.

I must insist upon this, my friend.

No problem, Leonard said.

Perhaps I owe you an explanation, Mill said.

I don't think so, Leonard said.

One day I intend to find men expert in the production of Cathay noodles. I shall bring them to Venice and become richer than the Great Khan. My father and uncle have no taste for them, but I was always the visionary in the family. Tell no one, I pray! No one must know about the noodles!

More about the clapping song

Carol's book group started meeting two or three times a week. From Leonard's room in the garage apartment, he and Felix would watch Carol in her black climbing suit, dust cap tamping down her afro, tie a large clutchbag to her Roadster and cycle off. She'd stopped cooking, just left piles of Scottish food on a warming plate in the stoveroom—miniature bridies and tatties and skirlies and crowdies, depending on what she'd found easiest to liberate from Jack-o-Bites.

I'm tired of crowdies, Felix complained. He wouldn't leave the window.

Shall we make a fire? Leonard asked.

No, Felix said, and hung his head. I don't want a fire, I don't want anything.

You can show me your opus, Leonard said. I'd like to see it.

Mom put a tire iron in her clutchbag—why would her book group need a tire iron?

They're probably doing show-and-tell, Leonard said.

Will she be back before curfew?

She always is, Leonard said, though these days she never was.

Destabilizing forces of chaos blew up a Heraclitan Grill, did you hear? After hours, no one was hurt.

I hear it didn't really happen, Leonard said, who'd heard no such thing.

I don't want Mommy blown up.

You can't get blown up reading books, Leonard said.

Okay, Felix said. Okay.

He left the window and surprised Leonard by getting into his lap.

Tell me a story, he said.

Felix was a boy of routine. He never asked for stories at night, only after school. He leaned back against Leonard and put his thumb in his mouth.

Sure, Leonard said. Who should the story be about?

I don't care, Felix said, looking away. You decide.

What about Princess Celeste?

Celeste sucks.

Okay, Celestina, then. Where does she live, do you think?

I don't care, Felix said. I don't care where she lives. I don't care about anything.

Do you want to talk about it?

I want to hear a story.

Leonard had to do something. Felix hadn't been able to wait for the Time between Here and There, he hadn't been able to wait for a story. He started to tell Felix about Milione, about the many places Mill had seen, the many things he'd done.

Felix stopped him.

He's crazy, you said, right?

Well, yeah, Leonard said.

So he didn't really do all those things.

Right, yeah, Leonard said. But it makes a good story, right?

Maybe, Felix said without enthusiasm, and put his thumb back in his mouth.

Leonard was at a loss. He didn't know any stories! He couldn't share Grandfather's books—they were shut tight behind sixty-day sealant. Felix sighed, deeply. So Leonard taught him the clapping song, complete with the dance that went with it. He probably shouldn't have. He was breaking the promise he'd made to his grandfather—sort of—and the one he hadn't quite made to his sister.

Felix seemed to enjoy it: pink returned to his cheeks, rather as if he'd engaged in five minutes of awesome karate kicks. After they'd sung and danced the clapping song, Leonard told Felix the story that went with it. At times he could remember only the line he was speaking at that moment, but as soon as he spoke it, another came to take its place. This wasn't surprising: every day for ten years he'd sat with his grandfather while Carol worked. When he got home from school, he helped his grandfather to the toilet, then brought him a snack—usually canned peaches, sometimes herring with sour cream. Then he did his homework on the old man's settee, and when he'd finished, his grandfather would say, Listen, boychik, I need you to listen good, and he would pick one of his stories (he only had a few) and he would tell it, and after he told it he would say, You're a good egg, boychik, you tell no one about this except your grandson.

He always told his stories the very same way, using the exact same words each time. Leonard couldn't help but memorize them, though this didn't diminish the pleasure they gave him.

At first. By the time he was fifteen, Leonard had little use for his grandfather's stories, little use for his grandfather; he was bothered by the old man's smell, he didn't like answering questions about school, questions that were increasingly confused, the answers to which (no he hadn't learned anything, no he had no friends) he found embarrassing. He definitely didn't like taking his grandfather to the toilet. So that when, on his fifteenth birthday, his grandfather asked him again if he could read the scrawls on his wall, Leonard, feeling bad for not being able to read them, for always being unable to read them, said bad things, unkind things. And then, two days later, his grandfather died.

Leonard felt then as if he'd been dropped from the earth. Milione spoke of a desert. Leonard could well imagine this—shaded by nothing, light always shining in your eyes, an accusatory light reminding you that you'd acted badly, your grandfather had died because of you, and now you're alone, you'll always be alone. Fifteen-year-old Leonard stopped speaking, he spent long hours on his grandfather's settee staring at the wall, trying without success to understand the script his grandfather had scrawled there.

I could have asked him what it meant, he told himself, as Medusa, a kitten then, purred on his lap. I could have asked him and I didn't; now I'll never know. I could have laughed at his jokes about herring—would it have killed me to laugh at his jokes?

Carol seemed to understand. She stopped making him do things he didn't want to do, like go to school, like go anywhere, really.

For five years, Leonard did little or nothing but follow the doings of Sue & Susheela, let Medusa in and out of the garage apartment, and care for Felix. Till Carol told him he had to get a job.

Like all of his grandfather's stories, the one that went with the clapping song didn't make much sense—his grandfather had learned it from his grandfather, who'd learned it from his grandfather (and so on), so maybe that was to be expected. But it was about demons (who cause havoc only on Mondays), so Felix pronounced it truly grand. His favorite was Kafkaphony, the demon with two wives: with one wife, he had leper babies; with the other, two-headed babies who fought each other and had open sores on their faces. He also liked Kafsephony, whose babies leapt from one end of the ether to the other, sometimes appearing as men and telling the future. Also, he liked the fact that dogs were formed in the ether out of bad deeds; they barked and howled, and bit people; they could find no cure for their condition till they died and were reborn as something else. He couldn't wait to draw the goats who look like people. And so on.

Can I really not tell Mom? Felix asked. His cheeks were still pink from the exertion of hopping skipping jumping west south north east around the invisible circle.

Grandpa made me promise, Leonard said. No one can know, just you and me.

Felix considered this a moment, twirling a lock of his red afro.

What if I add the demons to my opus?

They have to stay between us. You can show your grandson. He's the only person who can see it.

Will I have a grandson? he asked.

Of course, Leonard said.

You don't, Felix said.

You're better than I am.

I am?

Of course you are! Look at you! Leonard said. You're strong! You do awesome karate kicks. You have an opus!

I do, don't I?

And you've got red hair, Leonard said. Girls love red hair.

They don't seem to, Felix said. He was thinking of Celeste, whose idea it had been most recently to dump him on the municipal compost heap.

Trust me, Leonard said, and Felix did.

A pleasing style

Good news! Milione said one night, his voice again bright. A gentleman has arrived who wishes to transcribe my adventures. He remembers me from Acre, he has a pleasing style. A certain Rustichello of Pisa—perhaps he lives near you?

I don't think so, Leonard said.

Have you encountered his romances?

Not my cuppa tea.

He writes in French, Mill said. I gather this is the language for romance.

I wouldn't know, Leonard said.

I neither, Mill said. But he proposes to make me famous beyond the walls of this shit-piss town. They will have to release me then, don't you think? Really, I believe I shall go mad here.

Leonard couldn't argue with that. But he didn't think Mill's "memoirs" would help him out of his loony bin; they might occupy him, however, and stave off what seemed a deepening depression.

What will you write about? Leonard asked. I'd say no to the dates and silks, yes to the starving caliph and marauding khan.

I shall talk of the Tibetans! Mill said triumphantly, and the line, predictably, went dead.

The Desert of Lop

Do you ever feel you are the only person in the universe? Mill asked the next night. When the moon disappears, and the sky is black and the sea is still and there is nothing around you but the void, then, dear Leonard, do you sometimes feel alone?

I guess I felt like that when my grandfather died. Carol was glad. She was tired of taking care of him. I was fifteen. I felt alone then.

An orphan is always alone. I was an orphan for fifteen years.

So you said, Leonard said, thinking, You were never an orphan, you know nothing about being an orphan.

There is a desert of which I have oft tried to speak, Mill said.

The Desert of Lop, Leonard said, surprised that their connection wasn't severed.

Yes, that place. I was lost there, did I tell you?

No.

That is because I have told no one. No one knows of this. I became separated from my fellows there. The desert was full of apparitions, sounds that beckon—one hears voices there, the sounds of waterfalls, of livestock and bandits. You follow those sounds, or you run from them, it does not matter, you only ever find yourself alone. Within hours your brain empties, the inside of your head feels hot, as if filled with desert sand, your eyes become parched, your throat closes, you feel certain you will never speak again, and how could you, for you have lost all words. And there is no one there with whom to speak, nor will there ever be. Everywhere is light, but this light, it illuminates nothing! You are your inside, your outside is in, and you are as empty as can be. You are sere. Do you know whereof I speak, dear Leonard?

Maybe, Leonard whispered.

Nothing is more terrifying. It was like this for hours, days perhaps—it is hard to know because there was no night or day there, or maybe I was unable to discern the difference. A minute felt like hours, an hour passed like a drop of rain. The sunshine felt like mud, I could barely lift my feet. I walked, or maybe I sat, I dreamed, maybe I was covered with sand, or maybe the wind uncovered me, I do not know. I may even have died: this is not impossible. It is possible to die, then live again.

Leonard didn't know what to say.

I opened my eyes, and there they were. The people whose name I dare not mention, of whom I have not spoken.

Even Leonard dared not say the Tibetans.

Yes, Mill said, as if reading Leonard's mind. They were many. They wore silks, they wore garlands, they were like angels, riding on steeds with hooves adapted to the desert, steeds that flew across the sands. They took me to their tents, their huts, oh I'm too tired to properly describe them, but maybe you can see them, dear Leonard.

I can!

They administered potions and unguents, they put drops in my eyes. I saw things, dear friend, too horrible to mention, too beautiful to describe. My waking hours were as sleep, my sleep more vivid than any life. It was then that they taught me, or rather it was through their example that I learned, for they assumed I already knew. They saw how strange I was, how I had come from far away, they assumed I was like them. They are separated from their kind by vast distances, you see. But I think that is all I will say for today. Leonard?

Yes, Milione?

I have been in battle, I have crossed the raging seas, I have relied on my fellows and with them I have survived every hardship known to man, sorrows such as I hope you never experience. But you alone have become my friend.

Really? Leonard said.

You have an ability ..., Mill said.

To listen? Leonard asked.

Yes, Mill said. To listen.

Rusty's manner

Mill had all but abandoned his nighttime tales. These days he spoke only of Rusty, the poncy blowhard who'd undertaken to write his history.

I do not like his manner, Leonardo. He will not speak plainly. With him it is always You must take it as a fact, or I assure you most heartily that, or I will give over my wife to you should you find that it is not as I say ... When a man speaks in such a manner, I know he lies!

His ideas about what might interest a reader are most peculiar! he said on another occasion. I promise you, the only thing worth recording is these desert adventures of which I have not yet fully spoken. Others will soon return from the lands you have heard me describe; they will recount the customs there—this will happen sooner than you think, and quickly my little book will disappear. But only I can describe the marvels I saw in that desert place, the things I learned to do there. Rustichello is stubborn, however: he will not hear of it! If I write what you say, says he, the world shall call us crazy and foolish and, he is at pains to remind me, he is neither crazy nor a fool. What he wants, though he will not admit it, is to win back his place at court. He cannot stop talking about Edward of England, though what a king would want with such a man, I cannot say.

What does he want to write about? Leonard asked.

Frippery! This is his entire interest! Wealth, excess, opulence—any evidence of riches. Ordinary riches are not sufficient. If I speak of a tower made of silver, he wants one made of gold. If I speak of a palace, he subdivides it into a fantastic number of rooms, each filled with gemstones and silks, the finest paintings, porcelain, and napery. A dinner for one thousand in his telling becomes a ten-day feast for ten thousand. The world knows ordinary riches, says he. No one wants to read about ordinary riches!

Who wants to read about any kind of riches? I reply.

But I misspeak. The knave has another interest. He wishes scandal, he wishes ... but my mouth can scarcely form the words!

Try, Leonard said.

He wishes ..., Mill had started whispering. He wishes ... an affair of the heart. He wishes an amour! Preferably with the wife of the Khan. But I would never! Molesting the wife of my liege would mean death! Do not fear, says he. I shall write it so that you may escape his clutches. In the dark of night! Yes, the dark of night! Wearing the garments of a lady-in-waiting!

I punched him, of course. What choice had I? Despite what he might now say, he landed nowhere near the spittoon, but it is his manner to tell tales that cast himself as victim.

He also has that fascination with war that afflicts those who have never experienced it. He quizzes me most intently about battles I did not witness, battles with no bearing on my tale. It must have been like any other war, I venture. There were elephants, of course, and arrows. People were betrayed, people died. His face turns an unhealthy red when we discuss slaughter on a large scale; he goes into his dank corner, breathing heavily, and scribbles.

There are some things he will not write about, of course. He will not believe that Cathay is bounded by a long, tall wall, fully the length of the country, so he will not write of it. He believes me when I say that cultured folk in Cathay drink an infusion of sticks and leaves, but he finds the practice disgusting and will not describe it. He will not write about foot shrinking...

Foot shrinking?

In Manzi, they swaddle a girl's feet so tightly her feet will not grow, but instead bleed and exude pus and foul odors until they shrink to the size of an apple. It is on such feet that the poor creature must hobble the rest of her days. The women do this willingly because their men prize small feet. This is the truth, I have seen it! But we must not write such things! he says. Stories such as this will upset the ladies! We must not upset the ladies!

He is a liar and knave, and would make of me the same! Mill stormed.

We can't have that, Leonard said.

We cannot! Mill cried.

Leonard has a subtle mind

It is an outrage, Mill reported to Leonard a day or two later. The man has been in his corner for days, his back to the rest of us, scribbling. I sensed some outrage was afoot, so when he was on the piss pot, I grabbed his vellum. Do you know what he has written there?

I do not, Leonard said.

It is too shocking to say!

Please try, Leonard said.

You shall take it for the truth! Mill said.

I shall not, Leonard said.

He has heard rumors of Princess Kokachin—all of them untrue! We delivered her intact to Arghun—or rather, to Ghazan, for by the time we arrived, as I'm sure you know, the lord of the Levant was dead. It is true that she and I developed a rare friendship, it is true that she was young and fair like a rose and we were many months at sea and she wept copiously at our parting, but there was no amour! The prince's women confirmed that she was whole!

And Rusty?

Rustichello has contrived scenes in which I look at her longingly and she at me; according to his tale, we sleep on the deck of the ship separated only by a sword (dulled, of course, in bloody battle), and that in the midst of a squall, when it seemed we might die—but it is too despicable!

He has gone too far! Leonard said.

I drowned his vellum in the piss pot, I had no choice, but the man is crazed, he says he does not need me. Did he need King

Arthur's approval to write about him? Oh, Leonard, what shall I do? If the world believes I have betrayed my sovereign, I shall never work again!

Your sovereign?

The Great Khan.

Well, that's it, isn't it? Remind Rusty that you work for a king. He's impressed by that sort of thing, right?

He knows I was frequently sent on missions by Kubilai, that we conversed often about what I saw when I returned.

Tell him more. Tell him you were a minister in his government, a Deputy Leader or something.

I do not know what position that might be, but I understand the spirit of your suggestion. You wish me to lie, dear Leonard?

Not lie, exactly. More like a metaphor: invent a position that captures the high esteem in which you were held. The position then becomes a symbol that expresses the truth of your relationship. See what I mean?

Your mind is subtle. I did offer invaluable assistance to the Great Khan in matters of salt . . .

Think bigger, Leonard said.

Nothing is bigger than salt! Mill said.

Sometimes Leonard forgot whom he was talking to.

Right, Leonard said. Then make yourself the senator of salt, if that does it.

I shall call myself Chief Emissary of Salt!

No, Leonard said. You must be at least a governor. Chief emissary is not enough.

The governor of Yang-chau! Mill said. I was there for a time. You know, they use paper lucre in Yang-chau.

That's a start, Leonard said. But we need something more.

Rusty's a war nut, right? Tell him about your fierce battles, tell him you killed many warriors with your bare hands. Make him fear you.

But I have killed no one! Even the galley I commanded at Curzola was captured before we laid eyes on the enemy.

Find a way to make the statement symbolically correct.

I understand you, dear Leonard! I understand you. I heard someone speak once of deadly trebuchets ...

Excellent! Leonard said.

A compromise

Rustichello and I have come to an understanding, Mill said the next night. He will destroy all tales of Kokachin, and I will allow him leeway on matters related to war and wealth. I have told him that humility prohibits me from speaking at length about my governorship or about my role in breaking the siege of Siang-yang-fu; he may mention these facts but I will not elaborate. Your advice, dear Leonard, has saved my reputation and that of Kokachin. Please, tell me if there is anything I may do for you—absolutely anything! When I am released I will speak to the officials who imprison you! I shall be rich then and all will know me. I will hire you as my advisor—you shall meet the Great Khan!

I'm good where I am, Leonard said.

I daresay you are not! Mill replied. But I have never asked: How is it that you have learned this mystical connection? You know that I have learned it from ... well, you know from whom I have learned it. I recall well the days in that arid land. You know I met others there from Italy, though they did not travel there by ship. One, a Spaniard from Saragossa, had settled in Sicily. He was a Jew, with a Jew man's beard and puzzling paraphernalia. He was freakishly tall and had a pronounced gap between his teeth. He juggled letters in the air. Look, he'd say, look! The letters are dancing!

Dancing? Leonard asked. The letters were dancing?

Letters are insubstantial, I know, but in that unusual place many things were possible.

Dancing? Leonard asked. Did you say they were dancing?

Another man arrived, a Greek obsessed with mathematics. He had settled in Crotone ...

Like Pythagoras, Leonard murmured.

I believe that was his name! Mill said. Do you know him? You have traveled perchance in the south?

Not likely, Leonard said. He's been dead thousands of years.

When the Jew with the letters met the Greek with the numbers, he wept. Can you imagine? You live! he cried. We are one! cried the Greek, and together they danced. They juggled letters and numbers together, making the most glorious patterns, which the people of that place turned into the most peculiar paintings, some of them made with sand. But you—how did you learn such fantastic methods of communication? How is it that you and I speak?

I just pick up the telephone, Leonard said.

You just pick it up. Fantastic, Mill said. No need to mutter formulas or turn this way and that around an invisible circle?

A what? Leonard felt the hairs in his afro stand on end.

You must be very advanced indeed, Mill said.

I gotta go, Leonard said, and hung up the phone. And did something he'd never done before: he took the phone off the hook, disabled call queuing, and walked out of his White Room in the middle of his shift.

The world was strange

The world was strange; the moon shone silverly on the safety swing, on which Felix seemed to have left some crowdies.

Milione knew about the circle? It was one thing to say he'd met Pythagoras in a desert, and saw a Spaniard with dancing letters, but the circle? Leonard sat on the swing facing the moon and held the crowdies out to Medusa, who was suddenly there. He pushed himself forward and back inchwise with his toe, not caring whether he dirtied his whitesuit.

A rare bird cried out in response to the swing's rhythmic creakings.

How could a crazy man in the Finger Lakes District know about the circle? What was the circle? He seemed to think the circle enabled mystic communication . . .

Thwack! Leonard felt a sharp thrusting pain in the back of his head and fell forward, insensate, into the besoiling mud.

Whagghes

When he awoke, it was still night. Carol had him under the armpits and was dragging him through the mud toward her house.

Whagghes, he murmured. Carol looked back at him. There were actually three Carols in the starlight, three Carols all in fuzzy outline, wearing black climbing suits and dust caps, clutchbags slung over three of their six shoulders.

What were you doing out here? they hissed at him in unison. You're supposed to be at work! What am I supposed to think when I look out my window and see a stranger swinging on the safety swing?

He knows about the circle, Leonard mumbled. Who do you think he really is?

If you can talk, you can walk, Carol said, dropping his arms so his head fell back again into the mud.

Am I wasting my life, Carol? Leonard asked, looking up at the stars. Should I find a ship, head out to sea?

Come inside for some chicory, she said. We'll talk.

The world is full of wonders, Mill had said. All places have their fascination, you only have to pay attention. Bravery is easier, in the long run, than the alternative. The alternative being loneliness and fear.

Leonard rolled and turned gingerly onto his knees, then waited for the yard to stop swirling. When he finally stood, the back of his head pounded like justice sticks smashing against a door.

Inside, Carol had disposed of her clutchbag and was now wearing nightgear, as if Leonard really had disturbed her sleep with his spectral swinging. She was brewing chicory in a large earthenware samovar.

Leonard thought she was going to quiz him on his outrageous behavior, leaving the White Room in the middle of his shift, but no, she wanted to talk about Felix.

He's the best boy in the world, isn't he? she asked.

Of course, Leonard said, sitting down in a high-backed chair.

We'd do anything for him, wouldn't we?

We would, Leonard said. Are there any tatties left?

We would never let anything bad happen to him, would we?

We wouldn't, Leonard agreed.

We would protect him no matter what, Carol suggested.

No matter what.

Good, Carol said. I'm glad we had this little talk. Chicory's almost ready. See you in the morning!

It is Isaac

I must tell you, Milione said the next night. Some days when I speak to Rustichello, I see someone looking out through his eyes. It is not Rustichello, for he is a shallow man; nothing lurks behind *his* eyes but lunacy and the basest of passions. No, it is someone else. Can you imagine this?

Leonard said nothing. His grandfather's eyes on occasion had slipped from blue to palest green, his pupils expanding, becoming one with the deepest dark: then young Leonard had looked into something strange and black, an emptiness larger than the world he knew. His grandfather would return then and say, Boychik, you're trembling, what do you see?

You think me mad, Mill said sadly.

No, I have felt this, Leonard whispered, and wiped a tear from his eye.

You understand! Mill said. I knew you would. Leonard, you are like my very own brother. It is Isaac, he confided. I know it is he. But why?

Who is this Isaac? Leonard asked. Why do you dream of him?

He is a Jew, he is blind, and a holy master of secrets—this is all I know.

What does he want from you?

He wants me to talk with you, that is all.

With me? Leonard asked.

No other, Mill said.

Do you know a story about four men who walk into an orchard?

No.

Do you know a story about demons in the third ether?

No, but if it is a good one, I will gladly hear it.

But you know about the invisible circle? You know what to do with it?

Of course.

And this is what you propose to write about in your book?

Yes, I will do this.

Leonard's heart began to pound. This was very wrong. Leonard knew this because his grandfather had told him so, and because the thought of it made him sick, a sickness he knew would never leave him if Mill did as he said. Only the grandson of grandsons could know about the circle.

It is a bad idea, Leonard said. A very bad idea.

No, Leonard, it is a very good idea! Imagine how useful it will be for seamen and merchants, separated as they are from their families! Imagine if kings could speak with each other as we do now, separated by immense distances: trade could be conducted, and wars averted.

Leonard had to think quickly; there were no Listener algorithms to help him now.

Have you used your circle and formulas to speak with anyone but me? he asked.

Not exactly.

You've tried?

I tried to reach Kokachin, Mill admitted.

What happened?

Nothing. I heard a sound like forests falling inside the ocean. It was quiet but for six days it deafened me.

And when you got me you were trying to reach someone else, right?

This also is true, Mill said.

Forgive me for saying so, but you don't seem very good at this just yet. Maybe you need more practice? So no one gets hurt?

Mill didn't reply.

You could write about this in your next book, perhaps? Leonard said, knowing somehow that there would be no next book.

Still no reply.

Mill? Are you there?

Leonard, you are a most trusted friend, and you speak wisely. I shall consider your words; possibly I shall do as you say.

When they parted that night, Leonard had no way of knowing he would never speak to Milione again.

INTERLUDE

BOYCHIK

A friend

The complaints returned the next night. The phone didn't bleat—instead, the usual clients-in-pain called complaining that they'd ordered *Neoplatonist*, not *Neapolitan*. Leonard listened, used approved nicknames and the Lateral Sales Strategy to good advantage, demonstrated largesse with Neetsa Pizza coupons, and gained a more or less average number of converts, but his heart wasn't in it. Where was Milione? Was he okay? Leonard was sure now that Mill had rerouted Leonard's calls—how had he managed to do that? Now that the complaints had returned, did this mean Mill had gone away? Was he in trouble? Was his invisible circle dance the one Leonard knew? Would he hear from him again?

He felt uncomfortably bereft. He had enjoyed their conversations, he had looked forward to them, he had found in Mill not just a client-in-pain but a friend.

Yes, Milione had been his friend.

He was surprised to realize this, because really, he didn't have friends. He sometimes screen-yakked with fans of Sue & Susheela, or other Listeners, using an alias or avatar. To none of these had he ever confided the emptiness he'd felt when his grandfather died, or his lack of skill with women, or the mystery of his grandfather's changing eyes, or his occasional sadness. With none of these had he exchanged fears, or experiences of orphanhood; certainly, none had urged him to be more than he was. Yes, Mill was a friend. But still he didn't call.

When the phone bleated a few nights later, Leonard grabbed it with unprofessional enthusiasm and shouted, Milione? Mill? And was deathly surprised to hear another voice, a voice he thought he'd never hear again.

Listen, boychik, the voice said. I need you to listen good.

Boychik

Grandpa? Is it you?

It sounds like me, the caller said, but it isn't.

I don't understand, Leonard said, tears already streaming down his cheeks. He'd spent ten years on his grandfather's settee, listening to his grandfather's stories: he knew his grandfather's voice!

Who is it? he sobbed. Why are you calling me?

Boychik, I need you to listen good, the man repeated, causing Leonard to sob even more. You saved the world, just like I ask. You did very very good. I always knew you were a good egg.

Grandpa! You're dead! Why are you calling me?

I tell you, it's not me, the man said, but I need you to listen good.

Who is it, then? Leonard said. Why are you doing this?

You did very very good, said his grandfather's voice. I am so proud of you.

You are? I started telling Felix the stories, I couldn't help it. He's so lonely! I'm never going to have grandsons!

You know nothing about the future, the voice said. Trust me on this one thing. On this one thing there can be no question. You will have grandsons, and more grandsons, on this there can be no question. That Felix, he is a good egg, he is a good egg and so are you, you are very very good to him. This is very important. Don't you worry about Felix, we talk about Felix later. For the moment I need you to listen.

Grandpa, I was so bad to you before you died. I'm sorry! I am so very sorry!

It's not me like you think, the man said, but your grandpa he know this, he know you are a good egg. Not to worry, boychik.

I was just a kid, I didn't mean it when I said you were stupid and horrible and smelled like herring and I hated your stories. It wasn't true!

Boychik, I need you to listen.

I am listening, Leonard said, wiping his face with his flared cambric sleeve.

You are not listening, said the voice, and he was right. You have the possibility to be the world's great listener, but you don't listen!

Oh, Leonard said. Sorry. I'm listening now.

You saved the world, the voice said. I don't expect you to understand, someday I explain.

I don't understand.

Your advice to Marco save the world, for the time being, this is what I mean.

I was his friend. I called him Mill. I was allowed to call him Mill because I was his friend.

Forget about Marco. He did what we need. He publish his book and he don't speak about the Tibetans. These things he know die with him. I need you to do another thing.

Mill's dead? Leonard's tears started streaming again.

Boychik, you understand nothing. Sometimes you gotta read a book, really, you gotta get your tuchas offa that swirly chair.

I don't understand. How do you know Mill's dead?

He live another twenty-five years after he get out of prison . . .

He really was in prison?

This is what he say, right?

Yes.

You listen to what he say?

I thought he was an NP test, or a crazy man.

Marco Polo, he die in 1324, live a very happy life. Three children, a sweet wifey, he is one of the famous men in the world: this is what he want, to be a famous guy, he get this because of you. You are very very good to him.

He died in 1324? What are you talking about? I was just on the phone with him last week.

This is the mystery, the man said. This is the mystery and it is safe because of you. He publish these things how he do this and someday, someone use them for evil, this is for sure. You save the world, see? We are very grateful.

Marco Polo, like the pool game?

You are not listening.

Who is this talking if it's not my grandfather, and how do you know Milione?

I thought you understand this, boychik.

I don't understand, Leonard said. This is what I've been saying.

Boychik, this is Isaac. Isaac the Blind.

Lenny

You're making me crazy! Leonard said. I don't believe anything you say! I'm not friends with a man who's been dead eight hundred years. I am Leonard, of Neetsa Pizza, I live in the twenty-first century, I work in a White Room. Why are you using my grandfather's voice? Who are you?

You will read this book and we will talk. Make special note of the suggestion you make. You find Marco's false governorship on page 206, his false claim to breaking the siege of Siang-yang-fu on the pages falling after.

The line was dead and the doorbell rang.

Leonard didn't know he had a doorbell.

Package, a man said. He was wearing a striped green delivery uniform Leonard had never seen before. Leonard put his finger in the fingerprint flasher and took the package. It was a book: *The Travels*, by Marco Polo.

No one called the rest of that night, so Leonard read. He read about the lands Milione had described. He read critical commentary about Rustichello, the stylistic and possibly substantive contributions that chronicler had made to the book. He read that many didn't think Marco had been to China, which he called Cathay (he had! he had!). He read about the apparitions that beset men in the Desert of Lop—but not about the Tibetans, there was no word about the Tibetans, or a circle.

Any crazy person could read this book and pretend to be Marco, or think he was Marco, but there were the lies that he, Leonard, had suggested, on page 206 and following, just as Isaac had said.

In case the book itself was a joke, Leonard went to the Brazen Head and typed, "Who is Marco Polo? Is he crazy?" He chose grinning compostmen to collect his answer. They rushed off in their smash truck, stopping to pick up infofile compost chutes all over Italy, China, and in between. They emptied their chutes into the Brazen Head's mouth; he chomped awhile, then made the following pronouncement:

"Marco Polo (1254–1324), most likely of Venice. He was the first European to travel to certain parts of China, or so he said. The Brazen Head has difficulty with this claim, as the gentleman did not in his *Travels* mention the Great Wall, or tea, or foot-binding. He also makes dubious claims that aggrandize his position, which the Brazen Head cannot confirm through reference to ancient Chinese sources. On his return to Europe he was made a 'gentleman commander' of a Venetian galley and promptly imprisoned by the Genovese, possibly following the Battle of Curzola in 1298. He spent much of his confinement dictating his specious memoirs to Rustichello, an author of tawdry romances. While possibly a lying knave, there is no indication that he was crazy. Sayonara, my good sir!"

As a goodbye, the Brazen Head spit out an apparently inedible tidbit, which might have been a red-robed Tibetan; the figure scurried offscreen.

Something Marco learned in the Desert of Lop enabled him to communicate through the centuries? Was that it? Something to do with the invisible circle, the formulas? Certainly he seemed to know he had the ability to communicate over vast distances, but Leonard didn't think Marco knew he was speaking with the future. And for some reason, this Isaac guy was concerned that Marco not share that secret; for some reason, he thought the secret would be dangerous in the wrong hands.

The phone bleated.

I tell you, yes, is a mystery, Isaac said.

Who are you, Leonard said, and why me?

Who am I? I am Isaac, son of the RaBaD. Rabbi Abraham ben David of Posquières, mebbe you know him?

I don't know any rabbis.

Of course not. I am known by some as Isaac the Blind. That is because I'm blind.

I get it. Please stop imitating my grandfather—it's very upsetting.

Your attention is all over the place, this is understandable, but I need you to listen. This is how I do that. Besides, I have to choose some way to talk. You like Marco's accent? English but Italianate? I work very hard on this translation.

You knew my grandfather, is that how you imitate him?

I knew your grandfather well: he was my pupil in Narbonne. At that time he was known as Azriel.

Was that in the Old Country? Leonard asked. I only knew him as Bertie.

Azriel was a good man, very smart, and powerful, but not always so wise.

Hey! Don't you say anything bad about my grandfather!

You understand nothing, boychik, but you have the potential to understand much. This is why I choose you. This, and I have no choice.

Choose me for what?

To talk with Marco, for just one example.

Why me? Why did I have to talk to Marco? Why didn't you do it?

Think, boychik! What do you offer Marco?

I don't know.

Think!

I was his friend.

Yes!

I was his friend.

And what do friends do?

They, uh, talk.

And what did you do?

Uh, I listened.

Exactly!

You couldn't do that?

I have talk with so many people, I appeal to their spiritual nature. Rumi, to take just one example of which I am proud. I became Shams, his great friend; I convince him to share his secrets through poetry no one understand, except those who understand. But I couldn't be Marco's friend, could I? He doesn't have a spiritual nature. The best I can do with Marco is a little still, small voice, a little Rustichello ...

You were Rusty?

I do a little ibbur. You know what this is?

Metempsychosis: your soul enters a living person so it can perfect itself ...

Isaac snorted.

... or help a person perfect his.

This is what I do.

Leonard thought about this a moment.

So this Marco, Isaac continued, he is a good but shallow egg, thinking only about fame and material things of the world. But you, Leonard, you can be his friend. There are other reasons, of course; this you will understand later, mebbe.

I need you to go now.

I call you back, Isaac said.

I won't pick up. I know when you're calling.

I find other ways. This is your destiny, Lenny, you have no choice.

Leonard hung up. Only his grandfather called him Lenny, only his grandfather could call him that.

A test

When the phone bleated the next night, Leonard ignored it. The complaints had stopped, and just as well, for Leonard was in turmoil. The White Room, usually so comforting, now made him angry. He didn't like being confused, he didn't want to be in silence—he didn't like it! It had to be that some rabbi who knew his grandfather also knew whoever was pretending to be Marco, a thirteenth-century explorer, and somehow this person had maneuvered him, Leonard, into saying things to the fake Marco so that he, Leonard, would feel later like he'd contributed to the writings of a dead man, while he was still alive, as if that were possible, but why?

But no! Leonard suddenly understood! It was a test! Only a parastatal corporation like Neetsa Pizza had the resources with which to construct such an elaborate Scenario! They had his Life Portfolio, probably they'd recovered sound reels of Grandfather's voice from the neighborhood webcam, but why? To see whether Leonard followed NP protocol? To see how he'd react in certain hypothetical, highly unlikely Scenarios? It could only be. And he'd failed! He'd talked with Milione for weeks—too late now to report the missing complaints, too late to report the unlikely Scenario for incorporation into improved optimal Listener algorithms!

Leonard was in despair.

When the phone bleated, he picked it up.

This is not a pizza test, boychik, Isaac said. This is your very real life.

I don't know that. I don't know that it's not a test!

Is your pizza people knowing the clapping song?

Isaac began to sing.

What do you want from me? Leonard shouted when the song was over. Leave me alone!

This will never happen. You are chosen, you must know this. You show not so much curiosity for someone of your ability: have you investigated my identity?

I don't need to! You're a crazy person in Marco's loony bin and this is his idea of a joke. Tell him I hate him more than anything! Leonard shouted, and hung up.

He went to the Brazen Head.

"Who is Isaac the blind?" he typed. "Is he crazy? Is he blind? Does he know Marco Polo?" He chose the cartoon spaceship to take off with his query. It landed on several fields and cityscapes, abducting terrified infofile "passengers," which it quickly probed, then discharged (via an escalator) into the brain of the Brazen Head, which responded thusly:

"Isaac the Blind (1165?–1235?) was a leading Jewish scholar and Kabbalist in Provence, southern France. There is no indication that he was crazy, though the Brazen Head thinks his ideas were pretty out there. Yes, he was blind, though they say he could see into people's souls. Whatever. He was something of a scold: he is famous for sending a letter to his followers, the rabbis of Gerona, and especially Rabbis Ezra and Azriel, in 1235 (more or less), reprimanding them for sharing mystical secrets with the hoi polloi (ho-hum). Like good boys, they shut up like he asked. He was dead twenty years by the time Marco Polo was born, which you'd know if you'd been listening. Ciao, baby!"

Azriel? Hadn't Isaac said something about Azriel?

The Brazen Head belched and a tiny figure in a caftan escaped out its mouth, looked wildly around the screen, and ran off.

The grandmother of your grandsons

The phone bleated again.

Lenny, the man said, I need you to listen good. You need to quit this job and do as I say.

Quit my job? Are you crazy? I prepared my whole life to be a Listener!

You prepared many lifetimes to be a listener, which is why you gotta quit this job.

Never! If I quit my job, I'll never get it back. Neetsa Pizza doesn't like traitors.

Understand: there will be no more calls, already you answer your last call. Now you do as I say.

Why? You have to tell me why!

The world needs you.

I can't help the world: I never leave my White Room. I like it here.

There can be no more White Room. Is time for you to meet her.

Who? Isaac, you're asking too much of me.

Is time for you to meet the grandmother of your grandsons.

Signs and wonders

Leonard hung up the phone. This Isaac whoever-he-was was too cruel. First he squeezed Leonard's heart pretending to be his grandfather, the only person besides Felix who'd ever truly loved him, then he gave him a friend and took him away, and then he took what was left of his heart, that very small bit of secret hope that maybe someday, somehow, someone who wasn't a child might love him, and he squeezed that too! All the while pretending to be blind! Was Leonard so obvious? Could anyone see into his heart? The world was even scarier than he'd thought. He slumped to the floor and put his head into his hands.

When the phone bleated again, Leonard ignored it. When it was silent, he picked it up and heard a sound like air that had been dead for centuries; it sent a chill down his spine, or maybe that was the sudden cold coursing through his room—a mighty wind, actually, a mighty polar wind. Medusa, the neighborly cat, yowled outside. Shivering, Leonard tried to coax her in through the cat-chimney, or even through the door, thinking she might warm him, but she wouldn't cross the threshold, nor would she leave off yowling.

I'm not listening! Leonard shouted, and the ground started to shake, the sixty-day seal on his grandfather's closet popped open, the opaque flimsies on his windows became translucent, letting in great light—and from the corner of his eye, he saw movement on his screen: it was his grandfather, wearing his worn brown caftan, gesticulating to a small boy. He and the boy were on the settee in the White Room, before it was a White Room, as the room had been when his grandfather was alive. The boy had a brown afro and a T-shirt that read "I Love Grandpaw."

Boychik, the grandfather said to the little boy, there will come a day when I will no longer be with you ..., and the boy said, Don't say that, Grandpa! I don't like it when you say that! and the old man said, Boychik, I need you to listen good. A man will come for you named Isaac. I don't know how he comes but you gotta do how he says. Remember this, because I won't be here to tell you! And the boy said, No! I'm not listening! and he put his fingers in his ears and shouted, La, la, la, la! The grandfather smiled and shrugged his shoulders at the adult Lenny, as if to say, Look at yourself! What a boy!

Had that happened? Leonard was shaking. This wasn't a Neetsa Pizza test, this wasn't the joke of a loony—this was real, whatever real was.

The phone bleated and Leonard picked it up.

What do you need me to do? he asked.

This is more like it, Isaac said.

We hate traitors

The room was quiet again and no longer a White Room. Leonard had opened the door and let in Medusa, who deposited a dead chipmunk by the cat-chimney. He was yanking the flimsies off the windows when the phone began to ring like a siren.

Yes, sir, Leonard said.

High Command advises that there has been a breach of the White Room.

Yes, sir, Leonard said. I have to take a break, that's all, which is to say, I can't work for you anymore.

Medusa jumped on his lap and began to purr.

It's not the Heraclitan Grill, is it? Our Listeners are never happy there. They come crawling back, but you know our policy.

Yes, sir, you don't like traitors.

You know the only support they get is a can of Flame-Off for if they set themselves alight.

I know, Leonard said.

Was it the attack on our pizza grottos? They're under control now, you know.

I hadn't heard about that. No, it's something else. I can't talk about it.

You recall that you signed an *echemythia* agreement?

I agreed to be silent about—

Our recipes ingredients White Room Pythagorean Papers soul tracing aptitude tests meditation scripts algorithms policies and punishments.

Punishments?

You signed the agreement. Keep it and you'll have nothing to worry about.

Right, Leonard said. I won't tell anyone.

We know about your true-ray blocker.

Goodbye, sir.

Don't you come crawling back! We hate traitors!

For the second time that night, the doorbell rang. It was Carol and Felix.

I saw the shades were up. You okay?

I quit my job.

Good, Carol said. You can watch Felix. Don't worry if I don't come back straightaway. I'm going to a book-club convention.

She was wearing her climbing suit and dust cap and was carrying not her usual clutchbag but a six-gallon grabbag over her shoulders.

Go on, Felix. Uncle Leonard will take care of you.

She pushed her son forward but he clung to the ridges of her climbing suit.

Don't go, Mommy! Please don't go!

Big boy, Felix. Clootie dumplings and head cheese in the freezer, lucre in the peanut-butter jam square jar.

She pecked Felix's cheek and, before he could grab her waist, slid down the garage chute and cycled off on her Roadster.

Come on, Felix, Leonard said. I have something amazing to show you: the White Room isn't white anymore!

Really? Felix sniffed. Can I wear my lumberjack suit in there? Yup.

And my peaked cap?

You can wear anything you like.

Wow, Felix said, trying to take that in.

We can de-white the walls, Leonard said. I think we should do that right now, don't you?

Can't go back there

While Felix was changing, Leonard thought about what Isaac had said. Go to the University Library. That's all. The rest will happen and you will know what to do.

What do you mean? Leonard had said.

Go to the University Library, Isaac said. The rest will happen and you will know what to do.

Oh, Leonard said. Will I meet her there?

Really! Mebbe you can trust me just a little?

How will I know it's her?

You mean, will she give you refreshment from a well?

Isaac was being sarcastic. Leonard decided not to ask.

I haven't left the house in three years.

I know, Isaac said. And tomorrow you will.

I'm a little scared, Leonard said.

Bring Felix.

He has school, Leonard said.

No he doesn't.

Then he was gone.

When Felix arrived back at the no-longer-white room, Leonard could see he'd opted for his rainbow suit and shiny slippers.

Good choice, Leonard said.

Felix beamed.

You having a problem with school? Leonard asked.

Mom's taken me out. I have to be underground-schooled with other kids in her book group. No more brainwashing. That was before she got the call on her red pocket phone and went off. My teacher said, Raise an ignoramus for all I care. So Mom called her an imperialist tool. I don't think I could go back even if I wanted to, which I don't.

Not to worry, Leonard said. I'll take you to the University Library tomorrow. You'll learn a lot there, we both will.

But as they commenced to drawing on the walls of the no-longer-white room, Leonard couldn't help but wonder what.

PART TWO
THE BRAZEN HEAD

The caravan

The next morning, Felix was up bright and early, while Leonard was still on night-shift time. The boy was wearing a little fur jacket and white pants on which he'd embroidered images of his heroes—mostly people Leonard didn't know, but Leonard was also there, on Felix's knee. Bleary still, Leonard made some cinnamon buns, put jujuberries in a chokebag for later, and left some mealie pudding next to the cat-chimney for Medusa. Then he consulted the Brazen Head about library hours and caravan routes. To humor Felix, Leonard had the Brazen Head fart his reply. He then gathered coins from the peanut-butter jam square jar and was about to usher Felix out the door when Felix said, You're wearing *that*?

It was only what Leonard usually wore—green army pants and a roomy silverscan overshirt—but Felix seemed to think a trip to the University Library demanded something special, so they went to Leonard's closet and chose a flowered climbing suit Leonard had never worn and a long gabardine coat that had once belonged to his grandfather. Thus attired, they made their way.

It had been three years since Leonard had left the house, not counting the Time between Here and There. There were no scripts to follow, no Probable Scenarios, no saying he wouldn't get dumped onto the municipal compost heap, or the adult equivalent, whatever that was. Aside from clients-in-pain, the Chipmunk Patrol, and the occasional screen-yak, Leonard had spoken with no one outside his family since the day he'd made himself a White Room. Until Milione. And Isaac.

When the caravan arrived, Leonard helped Felix up the ladder onto the back. Felix was fine, but Leonard was shaking. So many strangers! But the passengers hardly noticed their arrival. A man in a straw hat was talking soothingly to some chickens in a mesh bag, another was playing backgammon against himself and grumbling when he lost, a family was sitting on black carryall bags, looking dejected. Two teenage girls occupied most of the floor space, lying down with pillows and gossiping about a boy named Jet. Along the sides were posters introducing the Leader's new Chipmunk Patrol: a group of smiling policemen who promised to make every neighborhood clean and optimally safe.

You sure this is the right caravan? Leonard whispered to Felix after he'd negotiated seats amid some businessmen in shark suits on a bench that ran along the side. Felix consulted his fart printout, then, to be safe, consulted the Brazen Head on the navigation watch Carol had given Leonard for his birthday.

Yup, Felix said.

The caravan jerked to a stop and from below someone shouted, Suburban Shopping Mall! The two girls quickly stood, gathered their pillows, and climbed down the ladder. The man with the chickens got off at the City Slaughterhouse. Three men in shark suits got off at the Business District. All the while, Leonard kept his eyes shut and firmly squeezed Felix's hand. Finally they heard the University stop called, and Leonard helped Felix down the ladder and paid the driver some lucre. The driver insisted that they owed him more, because of the new security tax.

Leonard consulted the Brazen Head on his navigation watch, which called the driver a bloody liar. The man blushed and said, Have a nice day!

The sun was bright in Leonard's eyes—he hadn't thought

to bring a diffuser. Felix, who was apparently thinking more clearly, attached his to the visor of his peaked cap, then took Leonard's hand.

Fun, huh? Felix said.

Leonard leaned over a holly bush and vomited.

The University Walking Grounds

Thousands walked the University Walking Grounds, many of them from foreign lands, or so their attire suggested. As Felix and Leonard followed the signs to the University Library, they saw Survivalists wearing camouflage and offering samples of dried chipmunk; Heraclitan Grill flamethrowers in their characteristic fireproof togs; also, royal pages from the monarchists' Food Court, barbecuties from the Whiggery Piggery, even a few Dadaists (the latter didn't have a food chain, as the Dada Dinner Diner had famously failed for want of a menu). Neo-Maoists, recognizable by their black climbing suits, were the favorite targets of proselytizing pizza greeters: Can I interest you in a Neetsa Pizza? Leonard heard a well-groomed boy with a clipboard ask a neo-Maoist girl. How about some Pythagorean literature? *There's more to the world than materialism and class struggle!* he shouted as she rushed away.

The most attractive and confident young people wore primary-colored stockings and thick sashes of bright veneer, their hair cut in swatches—this was the style, apparently. Leonard felt embarrassed in his flowered climbing suit: no one was wearing patterns! If only he'd stayed at home, but that had been out of the question.

When they arrived at the library—an immense structure built in the late Domestic Imperial style—Leonard's heart was beating so fast his health meter gave a soft vibrating alarm. He steered his nephew to an engraved rockseat, where they sat.

I'm supposed to meet her here, Leonard said, pulling out jujuberries for Felix.

Who? Felix asked.

My true love, Leonard mumbled. How will I know it's her? And why would she like me?

Felix's eyes opened wide.

Here?

Leonard nodded.

Excellent! Felix said. Can I help? What does she look like?

I don't know.

That makes it harder, Felix said.

Isaac said something about her drawing refreshment from a well.

Who's Isaac?

I'll tell you later.

This satisfied Felix, so Leonard practiced a five-second Pythagorean meditation that brought his heartbeat back to normal.

Okay, kiddo, he said. Let's do it.

The Book Guide

Leonard's Book Guide was Sally. She was his age, which is to say, about twenty-four and a half years old, and she wore her light brown hair on top of her head in a waterfall of curls and headbeads. She was lucky enough to have freckles, which she accentuated with freckledot makeup. Her clothes were old-fashioned—a combination of the heavy materials Leonard remembered from his last year of school, which is to say, when he was fifteen, and the neoclassical outfits Carol had worn at that age.

Sally shook Leonard's hand and he felt electric sparks way past his elbow.

I will be your Book Guide, she said. Come this way that I may offer you some lemonade.

They followed, and Leonard liked the way she walked: it was as if all the air in the world belonged to her and made way when it saw her coming.

Pink, yellow, or green? she asked when they arrived at the serving station. She picked up a ladle, prepared to dip into one of three large wells.

Felix tugged at Leonard's suit.

It's her, he said.

I know, Leonard said.

Just looking

Do you find the lemonade refreshing? Sally asked.

Very, Leonard said.

Then finish it, please.

Leonard and Felix obliged, and she said, What shall be your destination today?

We don't really know why we're here, Leonard said. We're just looking.

It will rather waste my time if I can't guide you, Sally said.

I suppose we'd like to see whatever you find most interesting, Leonard said.

Sally's face brightened.

I'll take you to the Voynich manuscript! Check me out for three hours!

Leonard did, then Sally led them through the lobby with its vaulted ceilings and clerestory windows, through the din of the talking-books room, up a dark staircase into the silent scriptorium where pale undergraduates worked feather pens, down another staircase, through a hallway painted aqua and green, into a long, wide room containing many scholar tables. Sally stopped at one, retrieved a heavy leather clutchbag from a locked drawer, and on they walked till they reached a bubble-glass partition. We have to be absolutely invisible! she whispered, and blew on an antiquated breathreader. When the door opened, she pushed Leonard and Felix through ahead of her. More long hallways followed—and dark staircases, in which Leonard could now hear marching music.

That's Peter, Sally said, no longer whispering. He works for me. When he's on duty he pipes a military tattoo into the stairwells.

Leonard looked at her quizzically.

Don't worry, she said. It's a good thing.

I'm not worried, Leonard said, because already he trusted her, utterly and with his entire being, this woman who would be grandmother to his grandsons—and he wondered what he might give her, to show her his love. Milione had said women want only three things: wealth, position, and compliments. Well, Leonard had neither wealth nor position, not since he'd quit Neetsa Pizza. But he could offer compliments.

You guide very well, he said.

She ignored him.

They eventually passed through a wooden revolving door, marked with a sign that read *Priceless Manuscripts*, into a paneled room full of empty study tables. An old man peered at them from a curved desk that dominated the room.

That's Peter, Sally said. I'll vouch for you.

Thank you, Leonard said.

Peter said nothing, just handed them some antiseptic silk gloves and pressed a button, allowing them into a small room to the side.

The small room to the side

The room was small but opulent: stucco friezes of angels cavorting amid orchards framed the lower part of the walls; above waist level, the walls were painted with strange botanical specimens, huge plants with drooping buds, and roots that dug deep into the earth; the ceiling was adorned with gigantic gilt flames; and the floor was covered by a thick carpet of yellow, gold, and pink rosettes. Against the back wall was an elaborately carved black-walnut wardrobe that looked like it belonged in the Leader's domus. In the center of the room was a scholar's table with four matching swirly chairs.

The local Society of Cathars commissioned this room in 1873, said Sally. They wanted the manuscript to abide in magnificent surroundings. They are convinced that it is a lost Cathar treasure. They are wrong, of course.

Leonard nodded, not knowing what a Cathar treasure might be. He wished he could slip into the hallway and ask the Brazen

Head, but Sally said, Gloves, please! and stood before the wardrobe—for a long time, as if gathering her strength—then opened the door with a key that was already in the lock. Inside, resting on a green plush dais, was a book—small but thick, about seven inches wide and ten inches long. On a bottom shelf were other old books, leather bound and stained, covered by a dustproof cloth. Sally removed the cloth, laid it reverently on the scholar's table, and placed the book from the dais on top of it.

This is the only unreadable book in the universe, she said. It is written in a code no one can understand. Emperor Rudolph II of Bohemia purchased the manuscript in 1586, though it is known to be older than that. The emperor was a strange man who amused himself with games and codes. He collected dwarves—

Dwarves? Leonard asked.

Don't interrupt, Sally said. If you interrupt, I forget where I am and have to start over.

Sorry, Leonard said.

He amused himself with games. He collected codes—no, he collected games. Gosh darn it!

Sally sat down and looked flummoxed.

I believe he collected dwarves, Leonard said.

If you know so much, why am I telling you? Are you from the Cathar Society? Is this a test?

I promise you, Leonard said, we are just an uncle and a nephew interested in books.

I think you should go now, Sally said.

But we've checked you out for three hours! Leonard said.

Sally looked defeated.

So you have, she said.

They're doing it! Felix said. Leonard, look!

The two adults turned quickly to look at Felix. His small face was rapt as he stared down at a page opened at random.

They're dancing! he cried. Just like in Grandpa's books, quick, look, the letters are dancing!

No one's supposed to know

Before Leonard could see what Felix was talking about, Sally pushed the boy with both hands; he fell backward and knocked against a stucco frieze. Leonard rushed to stand between her and his nephew.

What are you doing, pushing a small boy like that? Are you crazy?

She pushed Leonard then. She was surprisingly strong and Leonard also stumbled backward.

Who are you? she shouted, her curls and headbeads trembling. Did you come here to make fun of me? All I have to do is press that alarm over there and Peter will come with his tranquilizing gun. He's a Baconian too, and we take the Voynich very seriously!

You're crazy, Leonard said. You just pushed a small boy against the wall because he has a reading problem!

I don't have a reading problem! Felix said. It's just the way I see things.

Then Sally shocked both man and boy by beginning to cry.

No one's supposed to know! she said, slumping onto one of the swirly chairs. How did you find out? Did my oculist tell you? Is he a Cathar? I knew he was a Cathar! All that talk about light and dark! I knew he wasn't talking about my iris!

We don't know what you're talking about, Leonard said softly, but if you're in trouble, we'd like to help.

I need both of you to leave now, she said, blowing her nose into the dustproof cloth. Leave your gloves in the catchment box as you go.

But, Sally! Leonard said. We don't know what we did wrong!

My name isn't Sally, Sally said. Now go.

Grasshopper legs and the world of the demons

Leonard consulted the Brazen Head on his navigation watch about caravan times and then, because they had time, brought Felix to the (Nondenominational) University Eating Establishment to get him a snack of fried grasshopper legs, which Felix loved but today would not eat.

Can it be the Time between Here and There? Felix asked.

Of course, Leonard said.

It's my fault, the boy said. I shouldn't have said what I said. Now you'll never get married!

You only said the truth, right?

Yup, Felix said.

I think she's a little crazy.

I think she's nice. I want you to marry her!

Me too, Leonard said, surprising himself. How about we find out what Cathars are?

Felix nodded and poured sesame sauce on a grasshopper leg.

The navigator watch didn't have as many options as the screen Brazen Head. Leonard chose the window shopper, then pressed Speak to Me and asked, What is a Cathar? The window shopper smashed fancy store windows, grabbed shiny infofiles and hid them in his overcoat, then deposited them in front of the Brazen Head, which looked at them disdainfully and said:

"Catharism, also known as Albigensianism, was a medieval Christian sect that flourished in Languedoc and northern Italy in the twelfth and thirteenth centuries. Considered heretical by the Catholic Church, the sect was all but obliterated by the Crusades and Inquisition; a remnant found refuge in our Great Land, where they now form a small but powerful faction. According to Catharism's dualistic beliefs, an evil material world stands in possibly eternal opposition to a good, spiritual world. Personally, the Brazen Head believes the Cathars to have been influenced by Manichean dualism, though the Head recognizes that in holding this belief it bucks all manner of scholarly tide. Later, alligator!"

The Head stuck a finger in his ear, wiggled it about, and removed it to find, on its tip, a little woman, who was chased off the edge of the watch face by a black-robed man with an ax.

Not terribly illuminating, Leonard said.

It's the demons, Felix said. Don't you see? The evil material world standing in possibly eternal opposition to a good, spiritual world. He's talking about Grandfather's demons!

Give a girl a present

Leonard hoped Isaac would call with a Plan B, so he dragged his grandfather's settee back into the no-longer-white room and spent the night there. Carol wasn't back from her book group, so

Felix, who didn't love being alone in the dark, slept in Leonard's room with Medusa.

Leonard wished he could get in touch with Milione. Mill was a man of the world: he would know how to woo Sally, or whatever her name was; he could explain what Leonard had done wrong.

But Isaac didn't call, and neither did Mill. There would be no Plan B, no romantic assistance.

Realizing that Carol might be gone awhile, Leonard decided he needed to conserve cash, so the next morning, he packed a portable lunch consisting of jujuberries, some bridies, and cold revolutionary stew. He didn't have any lucre himself, having given half his salary to Carol, always, for his board, and half to the pizza-greeter ministry. Now he wished he'd kept some: he wanted to buy a fancy sash or a swatch-cut for his afro.

We need to bring Sally a present, Felix said. So she'll like us again.

Her name isn't Sally, Leonard said.

Yes it is, Felix said.

He seemed very certain about this.

I'm not sure she ever did like us, Leonard said. She was just doing her job.

I'm sure she liked you, Felix said. Before she pushed you. What can we give her?

I've never given a girl a present, Leonard said. What do you think?

She likes books so probably she likes drawings. That book of hers had drawings. I could give her a drawing. What about a drawing of the demon world from Grandfather's story?

Whatever, Leonard said. Sally probably wouldn't even be at

the library, and if she was, she'd refuse to be their Book Guide. He'd had one chance to find a wife and he'd bungled it! Still, Isaac had said the library, so after Leonard had supervised exactly five minutes of awesome karate kicks, they again went to the caravan. When the Service Desk assigned them to Dora, Leonard gathered his courage and said, We really enjoyed our conversation yesterday with Sally. In fact, we weren't quite done when our time was up.

This isn't our policy, the Service Desk said, so Leonard said, The young chap has a gift for Miss Sally, and Felix obligingly waved the demon picture. His sweetest little-boy smile did not soften the heart of the Service Desk, so Leonard said, Dora will be fine, but first the young 'un has to go to the restroom.

I don't, though, Felix said.

Yes you do, Leonard said, and they slipped off, first toward the restroom, then following the path from the day before, through the talking-books room, past the scriptorium, down the aqua hallway, past the scholar tables, till they reached the locked bubbleglass partition.

Criminy, Felix said. What now?

I guess we have some jujuberries and wait, Leonard said, but they didn't have to wait because along came a brisk someone wearing a senior librarian skirt who said, Chief Librarian Isaac said you were to pass?

That's right, Leonard said. Both of us.

Right, the senior librarian said, looking puzzled. I don't know any Chief Librarian Isaac, but he had access to my headset, and into the breathreader she blew.

Wow! Felix whispered as they continued along without her.

Between the two of them, they remembered every dark

hallway and stairwell till they reached the staircase that played marches.

Peter! Felix whispered.

Do you think she'll be happy to see us? Leonard asked.

Certainly, Felix said, but when they arrived, Library Security was there with their noise absorbers and library sticks to escort them out of the building. As Sally watched and bit her nails, Leonard's and Felix's hands were tied behind their backs and they were led exactly down the route whence they'd come, but not before Felix managed to drop his drawing of the demon world before Peter's desk.

A non-bleating, non-sirening call

That night as Leonard again waited on his grandfather's settee for word of Plan B, he got a call. He very nearly answered with his Neetsa Pizza script: those had been the only calls he'd ever received on a non-bleating, non-sirening phone.

It was Sally, or whatever her name was.

What do you want from me? she asked.

How did you know where to call? Leonard asked back.

The boy, he put your number on the drawing. Where did he get it?

The drawing? He made it. For you. To say he was sorry for whatever we did.

Yes, but where did he get it?

Too late, Leonard realized that he shouldn't have allowed Felix to give her part of his opus: it referred to demon stories he wasn't supposed to share.

I can't tell you, Leonard said simply, deciding that if Sally was to be his wife, he must be honest with her.

You're Baconians, aren't you? she whispered. I was wrong about you.

We're nothing, Leonard said. We don't know what Baconians are. We're not Cathars, either. I'm Pythagorean, and the boy is half Jacobin, sort of. You know, it wasn't necessary to tie his hands. You frightened him. We had to spend twenty minutes in the University Eating Establishment waiting for his health meter to normalize.

I think you'd better come down here.

Where? The library? Felix is sleeping. It's three in the morning.

Tomorrow, then. Come to the side entrance, the one with the sun on it. Be there at noon.

Will you tell me your real name?

But she was gone.

Baconians

Leonard asked his screen Brazen Head what a Baconian was. He was too tired to choose an information-gathering method, so he got the stock figure of a woman checking her watch and tapping her foot in irritated boredom, then the Head appeared and said, "You're joking, right? Sounds like bacon and onion, maybe a made-up word for an unappetizing omelet? Another time, key lime."

Maybe the girl really was crazy.

We have a second chance, Leonard advised Felix the next

morning. A third chance. We'd better look trim and act sharp.

He straightened Felix's peaked cap, wiped cinnamon bun off his cheek.

Have you been brushing your teeth since your mom left? he asked.

More or less, Felix said.

What about baths? Have you taken a bath?

I don't get dirty, Felix said. I don't like dirt, remember?

Sounds good, Leonard said. Five minutes of karate kicks, okay?

Then Leonard fossicked for lucre and packed a lunch—what was left of the skirlies, and some jujuberries. He had no primary-colored stockings to wear, and no sashes, thick or thin, but he did find a nonpatterned tunic in a robust lavender. It would have to do.

The caravan was delayed. The Brazen Head on Leonard's navigator watch explained that this was because of explosions the night before in three Business District eateries—a Neetsa Pizza, a Heraclitan Grill, and a Whiggery Piggery. Some of the roads had become impassable. The culprits had cleverly disassembled all the neighborhood webcams, so their identity was not known. Heraclitans (naturally) blamed the Pythagoreans, who blamed the monarchists, who blamed the Whigs. No one blamed the Luddites, whose machine-breaking bakers were presumed not to know about webcams. The caravan had to detour around the Business District—already Leonard and Felix were late.

They hurried through the University Walking Grounds, Leonard holding Felix's hand because he could see fights breaking out between pizza greeters and flamethrowers, royal pages and neo-Maoists. It was well after 12:30 by the time they arrived at the Library and found, in the back, an entrance on which someone had painted a crude yellow sun with spiky orange rays.

Sally wasn't there, she wasn't anywhere. Leonard wanted to cry.

We'll wait, he said.

She'll come, Felix said, and they leaned against the door, chewing on jujuberries.

Suddenly the door opened behind them and they tumbled into a dark hallway.

Shh! It was Peter. Quickly, he said.

Now that Peter was out from behind his desk, Leonard could see that he was terribly short, no taller than Felix, which is to say, about half Leonard's height. He wore layers of checked suede— shirt, waistcoat, jacket—and walked, quickly, with a gnarly cane.

You should have come on time, he muttered. Miss Sally will be displeased.

As they walked swiftly down yet more dark hallways and up and around various dark stairwells, Leonard, still holding Felix's hand, took the opportunity to think about Sally. Now that he was to see her again, now that she had asked to see them, it seemed safe to contemplate her perfections. There was the matter of her waterfall curls and headbeads, her uniquely stylish garb, and the mystery of her name. Leonard hadn't realized how much he liked mystery in a woman! Because he was still in essence if not in employment a Pythagorean, he took a moment also to consider her proportions—she wasn't wanting there, either! Her legs were just the right length vis-à-vis her arms, and her torso, and her cute freckled nose. There was also the alien quality of her obsessions, and the way his arm tingled when she shook his hand. Yes, Leonard concluded as they approached the wooden revolving door, Sally, Baconian or no, Sally or no, was perfection.

Closed for renovations

To move through the wooden revolving door, Peter first had to shift a standing sign that read, *Closed for Renovations*. At which point Leonard realized that the *Priceless Manuscripts* sign had been replaced by a crooked, hand-printed banner that read *Archive of Severely Damaged, Unreadable, Out-of-Date Caravan Directories*.

There's a new Chief Librarian, Peter mumbled. An Isaac Someone-or-other. No one's seen him, but Miss Sally wishes to take precautions.

Felix tugged at Leonard's outback jacket, but Leonard took his hand and squeezed it. Once inside the Precious Manuscripts parlor, he was surprised to see the room outfitted as if in preparation for a siege. Someone had brought in a small refrigerator and a hot plate and a tea service for eight, in addition to a crate of apples, a bag of dried grasshopper legs, and a large store of peanut-butter jam squares.

Someone has to be here at all times, Sally explained from behind the desk. Her hair was pulled back severely and contained in sparkling fishnet. She wasn't wearing freckledot makeup; Leonard could see now that she didn't need it.

Let's go in, she said, accepting antiseptic gloves from Peter as they entered the small room to the side. Inside, there was a cot, on the ground next to which someone had placed a torch-light and some books. Sally, probably, since her clutchbag was also there.

What do you know about the Voynich? she asked.

Leonard and Felix shrugged.

Have a seat, she said. It's time I explained. Don't be uneasy: Peter is standing guard.

For some reason, this made Leonard uneasy.

Sit, Sally said. People always sit when I give my talks.

She opened the cabinet and pointed mechanically at the book.

This is the Voynich manuscript. The Voynich manuscript is the only unreadable book in the universe. It is written in a code that no one can understand. Emperor Rudolph II of Bohemia purchased this book in 1586, though the book is known to be older than that. The emperor was a strange man who amused himself with games and codes. He collected dwarves—Leonard and Felix knew better than to interrupt—and had a regiment consisting solely of giants. The manuscript was sold to him possibly by John Dee—an English navigator and spy who shared Rudolph's interest in magic and the occult. The manuscript passed through many hands, eventually being found in 1912 by Wilfrid M. Voynich. Hence the Voynich manuscript.

The Voynich contains 246 quarto pages, of which 212 contain mysterious drawings. These drawings are of botanical, astrological-astronomical, biological, and pharmaceutical subjects, which is to say, they're of plants, stars and planets, and so on.

Sally removed the dustproof cloth, which Leonard noted was not the one in which she'd blown her delicate nose. She placed it on the scholar table, then carefully opened the book so that Leonard and Felix could from that distance see drawings of plants—book-size versions of the drawings on the wall, which Felix was about to remark on out loud, when Leonard, sensing Felix's impending irruption, pinched his side. She covered the book again with the cloth.

This is where my lecture usually ends, Sally said. Because this is where it gets interesting. The Cathars are convinced that the Voynich reveals the secret location of the Holy Grail, though they are utterly unable to prove it. They'd like very much for it to be so because they don't have much left in the way of documentation. If they can crack the code and prove the book is theirs, they might attract new members. The Strawberry Parfait ice cream chain isn't exactly bringing them in.

I didn't know—

That Parfait is Cathar? Exactly! They've got no outreach, no philosophy they're willing to share with their customers, and besides, once you're fully initiated you have to starve yourself to death, and who wants that? But Parfait lucre helped establish this university. They're strangling Voynich studies: they'll only allow research that supports their point of view! We Latter-Day Baconians and some other inconsequential groups have been forced underground, practically.

Baconians? Leonard asked. He couldn't help himself. He had to know everything there was to know about Sally: if she was a Baconian, he had to know what that meant.

You don't know anything, do you? Sally said.

Leonard and Felix shook their heads.

I'll have to digress, then, won't I? Roger Bacon was an English scientist, scholar, occultist, and Franciscan friar who lived from 1214 to 1294, or thereabouts, or maybe from 1220, it's hard to know. He was the most brilliant man of his age. He wrote the Voynich! Really, you haven't heard of him?

Does he have a food chain? Leonard asked.

No! Sally said, disgusted in a way that pierced Leonard's heart. He decided he'd ask no more questions.

He was a Master at Oxford, then he taught in Paris. We don't know where he was between 1247 and 1256, though I have my ideas. He became a friar in 1256, expecting that this would lead to another teaching position, but instead, a few years later, the Franciscans prohibited him from publishing. He eventually got around this through Pope Clement, formerly known as Cardinal Guy le Gros de Foulques, who instructed him in 1266 to write about the place of philosophy in theology. Am I speaking too fast?

No, Leonard said.

You have a glazed look on your face.

I think you're very pretty, Leonard said.

Sally stomped her foot. Her freckled cheeks became pink.

I need you to listen, she said. This is very important!

Leonard listens best when someone pretty is talking, Felix said. That's what he meant.

Oh, Sally said. Sorry.

Please, continue, Leonard said.

Where was I?

Leonard had no idea.

The place of philosophy in theology, Felix said.

Right. It was at this point that Roger Bacon produced the works for which he is most famous—and she pointed to some tomes beside her cot: *Opus Majus, Opus Minus, De multiplicatione specierum.*

Latin, Felix said.

Of course, Sally said. For the remainder of his life, Bacon alternately taught and suffered under house arrest, but this doesn't interest us.

It doesn't? Leonard said.

No, Sally said. Anyone hungry?

Code yellow

We should eat before I tell you the best part, the part nobody knows.

Jujuberries? Leonard offered.

Yuck, Sally said. Really, the only thing I like, besides legs, is, don't laugh . . .

Neetsa Pizza, Leonard said.

Sally looked at him with wonder and new respect.

How did you know?

Golden Mean pizza?

Yes! she cried. It's like you know me!

It's my favorite too! Leonard said.

We can order one from a greeter on the Walking Grounds, Sally said.

No, we can't, Felix said. He'd gone to the window, which he now opened. Sounds of mayhem exploded into the room—which is to say, shrieking, shouting, banging, clanging, more shouting, alarm whistles, and innumerable varieties of cacophonous song.

A riot, Sally said, as Leonard arrived to look over her shoulder.

Hundreds of neo-Maoists and food representatives were wrestling, throwing punches, and chasing one another around the Walking Grounds. Some carried sticks; others flaming torches. Strawberry Parfait soda jerks made rude gestures at pizza greeters, who brandished clipboards. Tapas chefs from Jack-o-Bites menaced scantily clad Whiggery Piggery barbecuties with kebab sticks. A tree in the middle of the ground was alight—the Heraclitans' doing, no doubt. Only the Dadaists seemed uninterested in fighting: they were ... yes, they were admiring a stoveroom sink propped against a jujuberry tree.

The music came from dueling musicians, established in different corners of the grounds—Leonard could make out the Heavenly Spheres rock band, some court troubadours, a suburban-peasant-worker chorale, bagpipes, and Whig fanfare, all egging their representatives on with morale-boosting melodies. Leonard couldn't help but feel Pythagorean pride as he heard strains of the Neetsa Pizza theme song.

The police are arriving, Sally said, and she was right: it was their alarm whistles they'd heard, and they were getting louder. A police caravan screeched to a halt and dozens of police jumped off the back, justice sticks and ID spray in hand, some still wearing their Chipmunk Patrol sashes. They began spraying and beating fighters and passersby indiscriminately.

Oh, no! Felix cried. It's Mom! **MOM!** he shouted in a voice so loud it set bells and sirens off in Leonard's head, and made the room tremble—then Felix was off, running from the room, Leonard after him, Sally grabbing her clutchbag.

Code yellow! she shouted to Peter as they made for the stairs.

Don't you hate that?

When they got outside they saw something they couldn't possibly have imagined: everything—every person, every breeze, every insect, even the flame in the tree—had come to a stop, everything but the three of them, and what looked like Carol's red afro escaping around a corner. A policeman's justice stick was frozen in the air, his face a grimace, a Whig's fist was immobilized two centimeters from a neo-Maoist kidney, and so on. Leonard stopped short, and then Sally, but Felix kept running toward the spot where he'd seen his mother. When he saw she was gone, he reluctantly returned.

What did you do? Sally asked him.

She's alright, Leonard said, taking Felix's hand. Your mom always is.

I want to go home, the boy whispered.

What did you do? Sally said.

It's hard to explain, Felix said. Can we go now, Leonard?

You've done that before? Leonard asked.

Only once. When the kids were about to throw me onto the municipal compost heap—

Don't you hate that? Sally said.

You too? Leonard asked.

It happens to all people of substance and quality, she explained, also taking Felix's hand. But you can't go home now, I'm sorry.

No, really, Leonard said, I think we should.

Did the policeman ID spray your mom?

Yes, Felix said.

Then he'll know who she is, right? She won't be able to go home; maybe they'll want you guys as witnesses. You don't want to have to admit that you saw her here, right? How long will this last?

Not sure, Felix said. Ten minutes? My health meter has to calm down first.

Let's do what we can while we're waiting, Sally said. Leonard, you grab the justice sticks, Felix, you bring that hose to that flaming tree, and I'll move people out of the way of some fists. When I blow my whistle, we meet back at the shining sun, alright?

She blew her whistle once for good measure and they were off.

A Baconian safehouse

When they reassembled, Sally explained that they would have to go to a Baconian safehouse for a while, till things calmed down. She ran upstairs to leave a message for Peter, who she correctly guessed was also frozen. Which meant uncle and nephew got to watch as the rioters came back to life, slowly, as if drugged. Some swung softly at the air, falling off balance to the ground; policemen looked vaguely for their justice sticks; musicians made halfhearted tweets on their instruments; food chain representatives began groggily to stumble toward the periphery of the Walking Grounds.

It's funny, Felix said. Like a cartoon.

Except it's not, Leonard said. Look: some people aren't getting up. They could be seriously hurt.

Felix hung his head.

Not to worry, little chappie, Leonard said, mussing Felix's afro. I don't know how you did it, but you saved your mom, and lots of other people besides. You're a hero!

I am, aren't I! Felix said, and Sally was back with her black leather clutchbag.

Come on, she said. The library's about to go into lockdown. I got out just in time.

And Peter?

He's barricaded himself with the Voynich. He'll guard it with his life.

Sally flagged a wagonette and gave the driver complicated directions for a part of town Leonard didn't know. The driver offered to read their palms or call up spirits of the dead, but they were tired, and low on lucre.

Another time, perhaps, Sally said politely, and took the driver's card. All wagonette drivers were mediums, she explained. Leonard and Felix hadn't known that: they'd never ridden in a wagonette. Dime a dozen, she whispered, but helpful in an emergency.

What's your name? Leonard asked.

Sally looked at him blankly.

Your true name, Leonard said.

Sally, she said. You're not much of a listener, are you?

Leonard was about to object, both to her inconsistency and her characterization of him, but already it was time to leave the wagonette.

It turned out it wasn't possible to drive to a safehouse directly. After the wagonette, you caught a caravan, then an underground railway, then you walked a verst or two, always turning corners and doubling back and looking over your shoulder. Only then could you arrive at a house that looked just like any other house from the outside except for a sign that read:

Brazen Head Enterprises

You're looking at the Brazen Head

Leonard had thought a safehouse would be, well, safe, with security guards and reinforced, steel-studded walls, but this looked just like a house. There was a living room with a comfortable-looking settee and padded swirly chairs and the ruins of someone's solo-game. Posters with curling edges were taped to the walls—one of something that looked like a star system, another of an old-fashioned man named Doctor Mirabilis. The living room led to a dining room, where a half dozen young people sat around an oval table.

Is that revolutionary stew? Leonard asked before he knew what he was saying. He was hungry; he assumed Felix was too.

Who's your neo-Maoist boyfriend? a boy with face spots asked.

We're not Maoists, Leonard said. We're nothing, really.

They're Baconians, Sally said. Though they may not know it yet.

You shouldn't bring just anyone here, the boy said, standing.

Shut up, Dwane, Sally said. Several of the others giggled.

The boy took Leonard's picture with his navigator watch, pressed a button on the side, and examined the results.

Leonard, he said. My man Stan! Leonard is interested in caravan schedules, Cathars, Marco Polo, and some useless Stan named Isaac the Blind. Why, you're a regular Renaissance Stan, aren't you, Leonard? Oh, Dwane added, looking more closely at his watch, as if he'd nearly missed something, Leonard has an abiding interest in Sue & Susheela. Hey, Sue & Susheela! You have a fan here in Stan the man!

From what must have been the stoveroom walked the very

same, holding identical blue dish towels. Leonard blushed all the way to his shoulders.

I admire your, uh, performances, he mumbled.

He wants to know if you're married! the boy shouted.

That's enough, Sally said, and to Leonard's surprise, Dwane sat down.

Pleased to meet you, Stan, Sue & Susheela said in unison. They smiled and returned to the stoveroom.

Pretty, Sally whispered, but not Dwane's best work.

You guys have been intercepting my Brazen Head communications? Leonard asked.

You hear that? Dwane said, looking around the table for laughs. He's wondering if we intercepted his Brazen Head communications! A couple of boys giggled.

I'm serious! Leonard said, emboldened by the presence of Sally.

Stan, you are looking at the Brazen Head!

Your inquiries got flagged, Sally said. You can understand why.

No, I can't, actually. Look, can Felix get something to eat? Felix? Where's Felix?

Bacon and eggs

Felix wasn't in the dining room, or the stoveroom, or the living room.

Don't worry, Sally said. He can't get out. He's here somewhere.

What do you mean he can't get out?

It's a safehouse, remember?

We're locked inside?

You worry too much, Sally said.

As Leonard took the steps upstairs two by two, he realized he wasn't sure whether he still loved Sally. There was too much he didn't understand, like who the Baconians were, and why they hated the Cathars, and why they needed a safehouse, and why they'd monitored his Brazen Head communications, and why Isaac thought this had anything whatsoever to do with him.

This floor has the Brazen Head, see? Sally opened a door to an enormous screen room. Leonard had never seen so many screens, one on top of the other. Incoming were hundreds of faces, all unaware they were being cammed. On the floor and on folding tables were plastic toys, as if the room were a children's playzone. And in fact, two young men sat on swirly chairs facing the screens. One played with a finger puppet, another with a handheld screen game. They looked up briefly, waved at Sally, and said no, there hadn't been any small boys in there, not for years. Unless you counted Gideon here—at which point Gideon upended the puppeteer.

Down a long hallway were several doors, each leading to a dorm-style bedroom. Some looked more permanent, with messy bunk beds and three-layer dressers, while others appeared more recently inhabited, with collapsible cots and cardboard boxes for storage. Felix was in none of these rooms.

The library's down there. If he's not in there, we'll check Alchemy and Optics.

But Felix was there, in the library, stretched out and snoring on a settee, Bacon's *Opus Majus* on his belly, a small cat lying plumply on the book.

That's Eggs, Sally said. As in—

Bacon and?

See, we do have a sense of humor, she said, though she wasn't smiling. Let me get you something to eat.

More bacon and eggs

They brought their dinner to the library so they could keep an eye on Felix. It might not have been revolutionary stew, but it looked and tasted just like it, which made Leonard sad. Where was Carol? If the policemen caught her, would she be branded and forced to live outside the city walls? Would Felix be sent to the workhouse? What was that thing Felix had done today??

If the boys are hostile, Sally said, it's because of the Schism—the wounds are fresh. They're not ready to trust outsiders.

The Schism?

The Great Split. You know. No, you don't. The Church of Bacon Scientist split from us some months ago—I'm surprised you didn't hear about it. They're in the process of opening a chain called Eggsperiment. It's mortifying. They're only interested in Bacon's empirical work, his study of astronomy and his inventions. They call our work mystification.

Sounds like my sister, Carol. She used to say that about Pythagoreanism. So you're interested in what, exactly?

Bacon's work in astrology, alchemy, and new ways of seeing. Dwane's in charge of re-creating the Brazen Head; Dravidian, whom you haven't met, is our astrologer; we've got a team of alchemists and optic researchers. We've also got the Good Friars in the abbey out back. We're struggling to keep them with us—they're only interested in Bacon's more orthodox theology; they think we're heretics. But if we can crack the Voynich, we'll unite all the Latter-Day Baconians. That's my job. The Voynich will make clear the essential unity of the Great Man's many interests.

I see, Leonard said, though he didn't.

I knew you would, Sally said.

Leonard stared at his sailing shoes.

I'm really glad we met, he said, unable to look at her.

Me too, Sally said. I feel it was destined.

Me too, Leonard said, and might have said more except Felix stirred, the cat jumped, and the book Felix was holding fell to the ground.

I had the most amazing dream, Felix said.

Don't mind them

A dream? Sally said, scrambling to her feet. Really? Wait, let me get the others!

What do you mean, the others? Leonard said.

Your nephew's a Baconian prophet—everyone needs to hear, and off she ran.

Felix got off the couch, somewhat groggily, and got onto Leonard's lap.

The dream was about someone named Isaac, he murmured. Is that the guy you said you'd tell me about? He had a message for you.

Leonard heard voices, then some shouting downstairs, and the sound of running.

I'll explain later, I promise, but in the meantime, don't tell anyone what Isaac said, okay? Not till we know what's going on.

Gotcha, Stan, he said.

I'd prefer it if you didn't call me that, Leonard said, and mussed Felix's hair.

I'm worried about Mom.

What you need is some exercise! Come on! Time for some awesome karate kicks!

Felix nodded enthusiastically. The voices had stopped shouting and Leonard could hear the heavy sounds of young men treading upstairs.

Don't mind them, he said. Five minutes. I'll keep time, and Felix began to kick.

A funny dream

One by one, as Felix practiced his kicking, two dozen Baconians crowded into the library. There were the half dozen they'd met at the dinner table, plus Sue & Susheela, plus more in lab coats, even a monk in a brown wool frock.

We're just waiting for Dravidian, Sally said. He's on the roof.

Shh, Leonard said, and pointed at Felix.

Several of the lab-coated gentlemen took notes.

Five minutes! Leonard shouted, and Felix stopped, his face pink and triumphant.

That was great! Felix said, and plopped back onto Leonard's lap.

Best ever, Leonard concurred.

Was that a prophetic ritual? one of the lab men asked another.

A breathless, wizardy guy with a starry cap and gown finally arrived—Dravidian, presumably.

We're ready, Sally said, looking at Felix with an awe that Leonard couldn't help wishing he'd inspired.

You guys really want to hear my dream? Felix asked. It seemed better at the time.

The lab guys all had their pens poised over mini notebooks.

Well, he said, and looked up at Leonard, who squeezed his hand. It was sort of like what happened today. All the Pythagoreans and Maoists and other Stans were on the Walking Grounds fighting each other, but slowly. I thought it was funny.

The Baconians looked at each other.

Is that it? one of them asked.

It was funny because none of the Stans got hurt, he said, looking at Leonard.

Sounds very funny, Leonard said, mussing Felix's afro. What a great dream!

He looked at the others as if challenging them to disagree. They nodded sagely, checked their notebooks, and filed out of the room, murmuring to each other.

Sally gave Leonard and Felix a cold look.

Let me show you to your room, she said.

Footsteps

So what was your dream? Leonard whispered as he tucked Felix into bed.

It was this guy named Isaac, Felix whispered back. He's blind, you know.

Leonard nodded.

He said we have to talk through the Brazen Head.

Through?

Yup, Felix said.

To who?

That's the weird part, Felix said.

Yes?

He said we have to talk to Roger Bacon!

The dead guy?

The dead guy!

What are we supposed to say?

He just said stop him! He said you'd know what that meant.

Wow, Leonard said. You did great, you know.

I did?

Sure! You're great at this dreaming stuff, and at freezing people. Do you know how you did that?

It's hard to explain, Felix said.

Can you try? Leonard whispered. And keep it a secret from the others for the time being.

I sort of lied before, didn't I? When I told my dream.

Yep, but that's okay. You did good. So, about what you did this afternoon . . .

Remember when I told you about the dream where four men walk into an orchard?

Suddenly Leonard heard a noise, the sound of tiptoes stopping outside the door. Under the door, interrupting the light, he could see a slight shadow—someone's lab slipper? He put a hand over Felix's mouth.

Later, he whispered. Everything's good, but it's time for you to sleep.

Felix nodded.

You need a story?

Felix nodded again.

I can't tell you any of Grandpa's stories here. So you'll have to help me out, okay?

Again Felix nodded, this time sleepily.

Once upon a time there was ... Who should the story be about? Leonard said out loud.

Celestina, Felix murmured.

Outside the door, Leonard could hear the sound of scratching pens.

Flapjacks!

Leonard awoke to the sound of someone shouting, Five minutes! He looked outside and saw most of the Baconians in a walled courtyard, doubled over and breathing hard in their gray exercise suits. Sally was facing them, holding a stopwatch. Again she was wearing a waterfall of curls and headbeads, though no freckledot makeup.

Anybody get anything? she shouted.

Everyone looked around, then shook their heads no.

Not bad for a first try, she said. Shall we go again?

A few nodded halfheartedly.

Remember, she said, we're thinking of demons, okay? Go!

Everyone started kicking the air, in poor imitation of Felix's karate kicks.

At the far end of the courtyard, behind the kicking Baconians, was a stone archway that Leonard supposed fronted the abbey. On either side of the abbey were turrets—why hadn't he noticed them before?—and in each turret he could just make out a man, in armor? And there, in front of the archway, a small group of monks—they seemed to be talking to a flock of pigeons!

Felix had arrived by his side.

They're all crazy, Leonard said.

They found a bathroom, where Leonard made Felix temporarily borrow someone's toothbrush. Then he watched as Felix washed his face and pits, then took the scrubcloth and washed behind Felix's ears. They went downstairs and found Sue & Susheela in the stoveroom, the only Baconians, it seemed, exempt from that morning's calisthenics. Leonard realized they were wearing the same skirts and aprons they'd worn the day before; the same smiles too.

Good morning, Stan and little boy, they said in unison. Would you like flapjacks?

Felix nodded with all possible enthusiasm.

Would you like jujuberry syrup with those or tree sap? they asked pleasantly.

You're not like any girls I know, Leonard said, looking at them carefully as they mixed flapjack ingredients in a bowl.

That's because we're not real, Sue said.

I'm surprised you didn't know, said Susheela.

What are you, then?

Failed models of the Brazen Head. Reworked by Dwane to be stoveroom drones and screen beauties. We're very pretty, don't you think?

Leonard nodded, then realized they weren't altogether there. They were stirring batter, and the batter was real, and they were pouring batter onto real flamecatchers, but tiny spaces were visible between their molecules, or whatever they were made of. It was disconcerting, in part because he'd once wanted to marry one or both. What had he been thinking?—but he didn't have time to ponder that now.

Does the new Brazen Head work better? he asked.

It is in good working order, Sue said.

The screen version?

Of course, said Susheela, smiling. You're not very bright, are you?

What's this? Dwane said from the door. His face spots were inflamed and sweat had left splotches all over his exercise suit.

Flapjacks! Sue said.

Neo-Maoist spies

We're very interested in your Brazen Head, Leonard explained when they were seated at the table. Or rather, the little chappie is.

Felix nodded, his mouth full of flapjacks.

Uh-huh, Dwane said. What about it?

Did you ever use it to talk to Roger Bacon himself?

You're loony tunes, you know that? Dwane said. I knew it was a mistake to bring you Stans here. They're now saying the police broke up that riot with slow gas, so I don't think young Stan's a prophet at all, he said, pointing at Felix, who, it had to be admitted, didn't look like anything so much as a small, sloppy boy with crumbs on his face and jujuberry syrup staining his shirt. I think you're both neo-Maoist spies, Dwane said.

You didn't answer my question, Leonard said.

Do we use our Brazen Head to talk with someone who's been dead seven hundred years? Uh, the answer to that would be no. Anything else you neo-Maoist traitor spies need to know?

Why do you have guards in your turrets? What are they guarding and who wants it?

You're not very bright, are you? Dwane said.

I could have told you that, said Sue.

They're guarding the manuscript, Sally said. Leonard hadn't realized she'd entered the room. When you're done with breakfast, we'll meet in the library and have a chat, okay?

Abulafianism

See, I have this condition. You have it too, Sally said, looking at Felix. It's called Abulafianism. Ever heard of it?

Leonard and Felix shook their heads.

Sally had changed out of her gray exercise suit into a very becoming orange-skin gown.

I didn't think so. It only affects one in six-point-five million people, and most people who have it don't even know it. You know how people with perfect pitch are able to identify the pitch of any musical note?

Leonard and Felix must have looked rather blankly at Sally.

Give any musician a C note and they can produce an A. Their ability to identify and produce pitches is relative; they just need an anchor, a point of reference. But someone with perfect pitch carries every note inside them, for them every note retains its absolute, unique identity. They don't need a C, in other words, to produce an A.

Okay, Leonard said, a bit dazzled by the way light shone off Sally's frock.

Abraham Abulafia was a Spanish mystic of the thirteenth century. He worked with the special characteristics of the Hebrew alphabet—the meanings and sounds and shapes and vibrations of each individual letter—combining them, being present to them. By doing so, he became a great prophet of extraordinary powers. Someone with Abulafianism has a similar relationship with letters—or, rather, with holy letters. Hebrew, for instance. For us, each letter has an identity in and of itself that goes well beyond its relative function in a word or sentence, and we sense this. You've felt this, right, Felix? The letters seem to dance?

Felix's eyes were opened wide.

Yes! he whispered. You see it too?

Sally smiled. It was the first time Leonard had seen her smile, and he decided he loved her all over again.

The Top Secret part

Felix left Leonard's lap and sat near Sally on the settee. Leonard wasn't entirely happy about that.

What does it mean? the boy asked with a seven-year-old's earnestness.

It means we're special, that's what it means.

Felix let out a huge sigh of relief. Leonard hadn't realized that Felix was worried about this.

The next part is the Top Secret part, Sally said. You'll have to promise not to tell.

Felix nodded enthusiastically, and this was enough for Sally: she wasn't even looking at Leonard.

Because of this ability I've been able to read some of the Voynich. Don't forget, no one before me has been able to translate even one line. Bacon used a lingua ignota to write it, a language with a wholly original alphabet and grammar inspired by his visions and mystical knowledge. Because it's a holy tongue, I can read it—or rather I've learned how to go about reading it. It's a slow process, and I've only just begun. The first bit I managed to read concerns your demons, she said, the ones in the drawing you made.

She paused for effect. Leonard nodded, but Sally didn't see him.

I believe that during the Missing Years, between 1247 and 1256, Sally continued, Bacon was learning Hebrew somewhere in France or Spain when he came across some knowledge, maybe from the Kohen Brothers of Castile, about the demons of the third ether and how to use them to achieve a prophetic state—a state like the one you demonstrated yesterday. The Kohen Brothers were the first to introduce full-scale Gnostic imagery to Jewish mystic symbolism, though elements were certainly visible earlier—say, in southern France.

Leonard and Felix again looked blank, so she explained. You don't know what Gnosticism is, right? Criminy. I'll be really simple about this. It's a dualistic belief in an unknowable good spiritual world and an evil material world—

Like the Cathars, Felix said.

Similar! Heaven only knows where they got these ideas; they probably originated in the East, maybe with the Manicheans. My guess is Bacon was so shocked by what he learned that he joined the Franciscans hoping to discipline his mind back to orthodoxy. Still, he was a scientist, so he had to record his knowledge— though not in a way others could read it. He enjoyed his life and didn't want to die at the stake. Hence the Voynich. So now it's your turn: time to tell me what you know.

Sally's voice was so soft and enticing that Felix and Leonard both had their mouths open, ready to speak, before Leonard stopped himself.

Felix needs to go to the bathroom. Come on, Felix, I'll take you.

But I don't! Felix protested.

Kids! Leonard said, chuckling. Come on, Felix. You know what happens when you wait. He extended his hand, which Felix, reluctantly, took.

Sally was dumbfounded.

I'll be right here, she said, needlessly, as uncle and nephew left the room.

Looking like a baby

Once they'd locked themselves in the bathroom, Leonard turned on the water.

You made me look like a baby, Felix said.

Sorry! I needed to get you out of there. I think it's time I told you about Isaac, but quickly. Listen, and Leonard explained about Isaac's calls.

I don't really understand, Leonard said, except that it's all connected: Isaac, your dream about the orchard, the clapping song, the Voynich, even Milione's Manicheans! And we can't tell anyone about any of it. Not even Sally.

But I like Sally!

Me too.

I want her to like us so she'll marry you!

She'll have to like us for who we are, Felix, because we can't tell her anything. That includes whatever it is you did yesterday when you screamed. Isaac knows Grandpa, your great-grandfather, and Grandpa told me not to say anything, that's what he always told me. And now there's this thing we have to do, we have to talk to Roger Bacon—we have to stop him.

Okay, Felix said.

Sorry if I made you look like a baby.

That's okay.

I know you're not a baby, far from it.

Okay, Felix said.

While you're in here, though, why don't you go?

Okay, Felix said, and he did.

World peace and that sort of thing

Sally was waiting outside the bathroom.

I have a feeling you're avoiding me, she said. Her orange-skin gown trembled a bit.

Never, Leonard said. The boy will speak with you, but not at this moment. There are still some things we need to understand.

Let's take a walk, Sally said, and took their hands. Again, Leonard's arm tingled from wrist to shoulder, though he was aware that by taking their hands, Sally had separated him from Felix. She led them down a back staircase, through a storeroom, to a back door with a song lock. She released Felix's hand and stood in front of the lock so they couldn't see the numbers she keyed in—the song lock played the first few bars of the Sue & Susheela theme song! Leonard was elated; if Felix and he had to leave quickly, this wouldn't be a problem: harmonic-interval identification was a core subject at Pythagorean boot camp!

Then they were outside in that same courtyard where Leonard had seen the Baconians doing karate kicks. Leonard remembered what Sally had said that morning.

You said the guards are guarding the Voynich. So the manuscript at the library is a fake? Or did you grab it before we came here?

The one at the library is a fake. Peter made it by scrambling a few examples of the Voynich script, which is why Felix saw the letters dance.

Why do you guard it if it's a fake?

Because they're watching, obviously. They expect us to guard it.

Maybe you should let them uncode it. Once they realize it's nothing, maybe they'll leave you in peace.

They won't leave us in peace—they'll know it's a fake. They may be idiots, but they're not stupid.

Felix giggled.

Sally smiled at the boy, and Leonard realized it was a beautiful day—all gentle breezes and the like. Sally squeezed his hand and he had to do a five-second Pythagorean meditation to clear his mind.

Can you tell us more about your plans for the manuscript, Leonard asked, once you translate it?

I told you: I want to unite the Baconians and put the Cathars and other pretenders in their place.

You say you want this. Is this what the Baconians want?

I'm their leader, ever since I cracked the first line, Sally said.

Dwane was the leader before, when he was progressing with the Brazen Head. The Brazen Head was a preoccupation of Roger Bacon, but not his principal preoccupation. I always said it was a waste of time. Now what I want, they want.

Once you're reunited and the others are put in their place, what happens?

What do you mean?

Once you master the powers described in the manuscript and achieve your goal of bringing the Baconians together, what then?

I don't know, Sally said. I suppose I'll work on world peace, something like that.

Ah, Leonard said.

Sally led them to a picturesque bench under a blossoming pear tree.

You can climb the tree if you like, she said to Felix.

No, thanks, he said.

Sally turned from Felix, and it occurred to Leonard that she'd just tried to get rid of the boy.

It's a big job, running the Baconians, she said. The others are slow. Lambiekins, you're the only one who understands.

She squeezed Leonard's hand now with both hands, causing tingles to surge past his neck straight through to the crown of his head. I need someone to help me, she said, someone like you, and Leonard could see himself becoming king of the Baconians, or at least their co-leader, here in this courtyard, near this pear tree, with Felix by his side, and Sally, dear Sally, always near him, his queen, really, only then, as he met dear Sally's eyes, he saw it again, eyes that didn't belong, looking out at him.

A Plan

GET OUT OF HER! he shouted. I mean it! Isaac, get your *ibbur* out of her!

Suddenly the world zigzagged—it shot forward and back, leaving Leonard nauseous from his toes to his afro, and Sally, who had apparently not heard him yell, saying, as if for the first time, You're the only one who understands—and looking deep into Leonard's eyes.

Leonard closed his eyes, so he wouldn't have to gaze into eyes-that-weren't-Sally's. And discovered within himself a Plan.

The boy would like to see how the Brazen Head works, he said, when he'd reopened his eyes. Felix nodded obligingly.

I'll tell Dwane, Sally said, taking Leonard's other hand.

Now, Leonard said. Felix wants to see it now.

Sally looked at Leonard rather coldly.

Of course, she said, releasing his hands. Follow me, and the three went back inside.

Dwane and a few others were in the Brazen Head room. Sally explained what Felix wanted, and Dwane said, No.

You have no choice, Sally said.

He gave her a dark look and proceeded to explain the workings of the Head. The many screens made the system look more complicated than it was. Really, it was mostly automatic by now. Incomings flashed on one of the screens, and their requests for information were routed through enormous infovats. Queries about certain topics were flagged, as by now Leonard well knew. These days, all the Baconians had to do was create information-gathering scenarios to amuse their subscribers.

Like the compostmen? Felix asked.

That was mine, Dwane said. The best ones are.

In response, one of the young men sitting on a swirly chair tossed a rubber duck in Dwane's direction.

It doesn't look like a head, Felix observed.

The one Bacon had did, Sally said. It was made of brass, that's why it's called brazen; it took him seven years to build. He thought it would answer any question for him, but he never quite got it to talk. We find a screen head works better.

How do you use it to talk to someone? Leonard asked.

You don't, Dwane said. Another daft question from our man Stan.

Leonard didn't have a clue how he was going to make his plan work, but he had no choice. No choice and just one chance.

Go!

Midafternoon tea wasn't much fun. Dwane kept giving Leonard the evil eye, and Felix couldn't stop fidgeting, maybe because Leonard had apprised him of his plan, and Felix didn't like telling lies. Sally sat so close to Leonard he could feel her orange-skin gown brushing beguilingly against his leg, and when he spoke she looked at him adoringly. Leonard might have liked that had he been sure it was he whom she adored and not the information she thought he had. Like about the demons, and whatever it was that allowed Felix to stop time.

After the jujuberry tea had been passed and everyone was nibbling a primrose tart, Leonard tapped Felix's leg under the table and Felix stood and said, I've had another dream.

Where? Sally said. When?

Sometimes he dreams when he's awake, Leonard explained.

It's a good one, Felix said. Much better than the last.

What? Sally said. Tell us!

I'd like to be in the library. I'd like to be holding the manuscript. Everyone has to be there.

Okay, Sally said. Hop to, Stans! Dwane, go ask the Good Friars if they want to send a representative. Hurry!

Everyone reassembled in the library; Leonard made sure he stood next to the door.

Is everyone here? Felix asked. If anyone's missing, this won't work.

Sally did a head count.

Everyone's accounted for, she said.

I need to do my prophetic ritual first, Felix said. Who will time me?

Twenty hands shot into the air. Felix picked an alchemist standing far from the door.

Five minutes, Felix said, and for this to work, I need everyone's absolute concentration. Watch me unwaveringly and think only pure thoughts. You ready?

The alchemist nodded.

You're supposed to say, GO!

GO! the alchemist said, and Leonard slipped from the room.

Speaking to Roger Bacon

He went quickly to the Brazen Head room and locked himself in. He knocked some checkers off a swirly chair and sat there a moment.

He didn't know what to do. All afternoon he'd thought about this, but he was still at a loss. If it had been anything else about which he needed information, he'd have asked the Brazen Head!

That was it! He'd ask the Brazen Head! He pressed the Speak to Me button on his navigator watch, as if the Brazen Head itself weren't there.

How do I use the Brazen Head to talk to someone? he asked, and chose the swiftest information-gathering mechanism: a simple riffle through a filing cabinet.

Lights in the room started flashing, because his query had been flagged, Leonard supposed, but the answer came up anyway, and it was simpler than he would have thought.

What a daft question, it said. Just ask! And so Leonard did.

I want to speak to Roger Bacon through the Brazen Head. Please.

A sound like an old-fashioned dialphone came from the screens.

Brazen Head? he heard an English voice say. Brazen Head, is it you?

Time for you to save the world

It is I, Leonard said. How are you?

How am I? I am speechless! I have long been staring at your brazen face, waiting for you to speak! It is a miracle! Where shall we begin?

Listen, Roger, I can't talk long. It is very important that you listen. Very important.

Yes, Brazen Head! I am listening.

No, I mean, you really have to listen! What I am about to say will change the course of history. You have a destiny, Roger. It is time for you to fulfill that destiny, but you must listen to me. You must listen very, very carefully.

I'm listening, Brazen Head! Speak to me! Do you wish to reveal the secrets of astrology? Optics? I have this idea for a flying machine, perhaps you can help me with that? Ships that run on steam? Exploding powder? I have so many ideas, there is so much to do!

You are not listening, Roger! It's time for you to save the world.

Oh, Roger said. I'm listening.

You are using your secret language to write a manuscript. I know of this.

Yes, I am.

It is imperfect. It will be used by future generations for evil.

No! I am using a method of encryption that no one can know.

I know, Leonard said. The letters dance, don't they?

Roger gasped.

You are truly a miracle, Brazen Head!

You must anchor the letters. Find a way. They must not dance. Do you understand what I am saying? The letters must not dance. This is very, very important.

I must anchor the letters.

Will you do this? They must not dance.

I can do this. Yes, I know how to do this.

You know how to do this?

I am Roger Bacon, the most marvelous mind of my age!

How will you do this?

I will use a different ink! An ink made of snails!

No, Roger. You must use a different language. Not your lingua ignota, not the language you receive from visions. Others who have visions will be able to read that language, and they will use what you write for ill. What we need is an unbreakable code. Got it?

Can you speak to the dead, O Brazen Head?

Focus, Roger. I have a message for you. Have you understood me? I may not return, so it's very important that you listen. I will tell you one more thing, something that will make you a famous man for all eternity. You must befriend Pope Clement . . .

Pope who?

Clement! Guy somebody or other . . .

Cardinal Guy le Gros de Foulques? He is to be pope?

Roger, I need you to listen! Your Franciscans will not allow you to write. Clement will allow you to write, but only for a short while. Use the time well, but whatever you do, do not write about what you learned in Spain. If you do that, Clement will burn you at the stake and your writings, all your knowledge, will be lost forever. I guarantee it and I am the Brazen Head!

What about the optical lenses I propose to place before people's eyes to sharpen their vision? Can you not help me with that?

Do as I say. Over and out, and Leonard ran from the room.

Sally wasn't clapping

Leonard snuck up on the library so no one but Felix would see. Everyone was fixed on the boy except Sally, who stood against the wall where she could watch both Felix and the door. Her eyes shot lasers at Leonard. He held his stomach with his hand as if he'd been sick and pretended not to see her.

When Felix saw Leonard he was visibly relieved.

Then Celestina said, I love you, Felix, marry me! The end!

The Baconians looked at each other.

Great dream! Leonard said. I heard it from the hall. Fit of gas, he explained for Sally's benefit. I especially liked the middle part about the . . .

The castle? Felix said.

No, the other part.

The ogre who tried to steal Celestina?

Yes! Gives us a lot to think about, doesn't it? What do you think, Stans? How about some applause for young Felix? and Leonard started clapping. The Baconians joined in, confusedly.

Sally wasn't clapping.

Where were you? she asked, when the rest had gone downstairs to debrief over some primrose tart. I know you weren't in the hallway farting.

Felix giggled.

Felix made me leave the room. I make him self-conscious. He's never told his dreams to a crowd before.

Hmm, Sally said, unconvinced.

I've been thinking about what you said earlier, Leonard said, about needing someone to guide the Baconians. I may be just the guy you're looking for.

Hmm, Sally said.

Show us the part of the Voynich that you've translated. We'll see if Felix can help.

This was an offer Sally couldn't resist. She took the manuscript, which Felix had been holding to his chest, and brought it to the scholar's desk. She untied the seven knots with which its slipcloth was fastened and removed the book, put on some silk gloves stored inside the slipcloth, and opened the book to a page toward the back, identifiable, she said, by a peculiar drawing of what looked like a woman in a bathtub.

Leonard got his first good look at the manuscript, and started: the script, while unreadable, was familiar, more familiar to him, almost, than the Leader's Revised Alphabet, more familiar even than Screen Slanguage. It was the script his grandfather had scrawled on the walls all those years before, the script he'd always hoped Leonard could read. He understood now: his grandfather had wanted to know whether Leonard had the Special Gift! It had to be! How proud he would have been to know Felix!

Is she nude? Felix asked, referring to the woman in the bathtub.

Levitov says this drawing represents the Cathar rite of the Endura, but we . . .

Sally went pale. She stared at the page.

Do you see it, Felix? she whispered. Please, I know you guys aren't telling me the truth, but tell me, Felix, please, do you see it?

Felix looked at Leonard. He nodded slightly.

Are you asking if the letters are dancing?

Sally nodded. Felix studied the page.

They're not, Felix said. Not at all.

Sally turned some pages, more quickly than was probably good for the manuscript.

I can't read any of it. What did you guys do? she whispered. All guile had drained from her face, and when Leonard looked into her eyes, it was only her eyes, bereft and lonely, that he saw.

He considered sticking to his original story, which was that the book had been with Felix, in plain sight, those few moments when he'd been out of the room, but he was finished with lying.

I can't tell you, Sally. I'm sorry.

She dropped the manuscript and backed away from Leonard.

All this time we assumed Felix was the prophet, but it was you, wasn't it? I've been such a fool! You saw right through me, didn't you?

I'm not a prophet, Leonard said, but I do like you very much.

If they find out I can't read this, I'll be finished!

What do you mean?

Dwane. When I started cracking the Voynich, I put him in his place. We've got to get out of here, like, tonight!

At that moment, alarm whistles began to sound.

MAOISTS! someone shouted. THE NEO-MAOISTS ARE HERE!

The three ran to the window and sure enough, neo-Maoists in black climbing suits were surrounding the compound. Inside the courtyard, Latter-Day Baconians were running toward the abbey and returning with armor and arrows. A few had begun climbing the walls.

STOP! Felix shouted out the window. Don't make me use my powers! They don't want your stupid manuscript—they want me! Anyone moves, I'll freeze all of you, and destroy your precious Brazen Head and burn your stupid Voynich and wreck your dumb alchemy lab and anything else I can think of!

Nobody moved.

Is she out there? Felix whispered. Can you see her?

Yes, Leonard said. I see red hair, over by the Brazen Head Enterprises sign. Let's go. You coming, Sally?

Yes, Sally said. I guess I am.

Susheela growled

Sally grabbed her manuscript and clutchbag, and the three went quickly downstairs.

Sue & Susheela were waiting.

We don't want to move, but we'd like to kiss the little Stan goodbye, they said.

That won't be possible, Sally said.

One was holding a dishrag tightly in her hand. Sally was right! What if they'd tried to gag the boy!

Send him kisses, Leonard said. That will do.

Susheela growled.

What I do, it works on nonpeople too, Felix said.

Outside, they found Carol by the sign. Her climbing suit looked a bit tatty and her red afro was matted, but she looked healthy and in good spirits. Felix wrapped his arms around her middle and held on tight.

These folks are from my book group, she said, of the dozen or so neo-Maoists who had gathered round. We wanted to make sure you were okay.

Carol, this is Sally.

Carol looked Sally over.

She'll do. I gotta go. I ordered a wagonette to take you home.

Is it safe? Leonard asked.

Of course. Casseroles in the freezer. Love you, jujuberry!

She kissed Felix and was off.

As their wagonette pulled away, the Baconians shot a few halfhearted arrows after them.

They're just trying to prove a point, Sally said.

A point, Felix said. Get it?

I'm sorry about everything, Leonard said.

No, Sally said, I'm sorry.

I really do like you, Leonard said.

Me too, said Sally.

Is your name really Sally?

Of course it is.

You have to learn to trust each other, the driver said, handing back a few of his business cards (*Elphadot, Senior Medium, Acme Medium Emporium*). You pretended to be something you were not, he said, looking back at Leonard, while you pretended to have feelings you didn't have, he said, looking back at Sally.

Watch the road! Sally said.

I have a message for someone named Leonard?

That would be me, Leonard said.

A blind guy told me to tell you, You did good, boychik. I knew you were a good egg. Does that make sense to you, because it sure don't make sense to me.

Leonard smiled.

INTERLUDE

BOYCHIK AGAIN

Hero!

A person could excuse Leonard for smiling. He'd done a good job—Isaac had said so!—and now he was sitting with two of the three people he loved most in the world. Sally, moreover, had no place to go, no choice but to be with him, which was good, because if she had a choice, she might choose otherwise. Life was good, and Leonard was a hero. He'd done things he'd never imagined doing—he'd come up with plans, he'd defeated an entire Baconian empire, sort of. He'd changed the course of history—*again!* Twice in two days, almost! Only a short while ago, he'd been Just Leonard, who never left his White Room, who solved all problems with conversion scripts and preapproved Listener algorithms. Just Leonard, too shy to be a pizza greeter, living by his wits now! A leader of men!

Exultant, Leonard watched the flowering trees speed by as the wagonette made its way through a dusky residential district, full of shoebox houses painted blue and green, Failsafe Guards posted outside the gates, some of them snoozing, which made Leonard smile all the more. They would return to Leonard's garage apartment, he'd give Sally the no-longer-white room for her exclusive use until they were married, as long as she promised not to paint over Felix's drawings on the walls ... Oh, joy! The sun seemed to agree, sending cheerful pink rays over the Industrial District, as it sunk behind spiraling smokestacks and liveried lorries. He wondered whether Sally knew how to cook.

Speaking of which, his true love was hiccupping! How adorable was that? Before he knew what he was doing, he put his arm around her and dared to look in her eyes.

She was fighting back tears; Felix was already squeezing her hand.

What is it, Sally? he asked.

She didn't answer; she only shook her head.

Leonard felt like such a fool. Of course: good fortune was his only because Sally had lost hers! Her Special Gift, her friends, her job, her safehouse—all gone! Felix had understood, but Leonard—Leonard had thought only of himself! How lowly was that? Lowly as a worm! Leonard was no better than a worm! What did he have to offer Sally? No wealth, no position. Nothing! Less than nothing! He didn't have a job, or any notion where to find one. He was responsible for a seven-year-old boy who no longer went to school, his sister was a renegade neo-Maoist wanted by the police, their home might not even be safe!

The sky was no longer rosy, it was streaked with gray. They seemed to be on the edge of the Business District, but it was smoky, and darkening, and hard to see.

Your home isn't safe, the wagonette driver said, pulling over to the curb. My wagonette oath does not permit me to deliver you there. Besides, you haven't the lucre to pay me.

Simultaneously, the three dug into their pockets. Among them they only had three coins.

I'll leave you here, then, shall I? the wagonette driver said, releasing the airlocks. Around them, the dusk-laden street was lit only by roving beams from unmanned fire towers. Leonard rolled down his soundproof window and heard, from not far away, the distinctive zing-hiss-boom of pocket rockets. And shouting. Lots of shouting.

What's going on? Sally asked as Leonard grasped her hand, but she was addressing Elphadot, the driver.

More of the same, he said. You'll want to avoid Main Street. And most of the side streets.

You can't just leave us here! Leonard said.

The police are at your house, he said, but they'll be too busy to bother with you here. Just avoid Main Street, like I said. And most of the side streets. Lucre, please?

The three handed over what was left of their cash, and as the wagonette reversed direction and sped off, Sally pulled a small round of material from her clutchbag, then pressed what appeared to Leonard to be a pumpswitch. The material expanded into a hat—a very stylish hat with a wide brim and cherry blossom–jujuberry motif. Placed on Sally's head, it illuminated a twenty-foot radius.

Stan the man! Felix exclaimed.

It's a personal collapsible beacon, beta version, based on Baconian optics, Sally said proudly. She took it off to show Felix, and they were in darkness again. It works only on my head!

Light, please, Leonard said, feeling jealous of the bond Sally and Felix were forming. At his expense, he assumed, though he couldn't say how.

Sally put the hat back on and they found themselves in a Business District none of them recognized. While the side street they stood on was quiet, at the intersection a quarter verst ahead they could see one building reduced to a smoking titanium frame, while another, to its left, was fully aflame. As they crept forward, Sally's hat illuminated bands of Heraclitan flamethrowers running through the intersection, chased by monarchist jousters on horseback and—could it be?—off-key singing waiters from the Dada Dinner Diner. Soda jerks from the Strawberry Parfait were shouting insults and trying to trip the horses. The street was cluttered with abandoned torches, eatery leaflets, and broken glass; neighborhood webcams and *Hello!* lamps had been wrenched from their Everything's-Okay poles. It smelled—not just of smoldering buildings but of burning pizza, blackened bacon, charred grillsteak, and blistering jujuberries. The musicians had wisely stayed away, but amid the exploding rockets and shattering glass and clattering of horses' hooves, they could hear, faintly, as if from an old-fashioned discograph, a tinny rendition of the "Internationale." In Chinese.

Mother! Felix whispered, and Leonard grabbed him.

No running off, Leonard said. And no shouting.

I think it would be prudent if we put the hat away, Sally whispered, and again they were in darkness. Shall we sidle to the side and make a plan?

A plan? Leonard was good at that! He would choose for himself a role that allowed him to be brave—brave but not foolhardy. He would protect Sally from danger—well, not immediate danger, but imminent danger, probable danger ... But just then, alarm whistles sounded, audible even over the din, and a dozen neo-Maoists, visible in silhouette against the flames and identifiable by their dust caps, ran through the distant intersection, pursued by police. One slightly built Maoist tripped on a fallen neighborhood webcam. As her jaw hit the cobbles, her dust cap flew off. A policeman was immediately upon her, beating her backside with his justice stick. She curled to her left in the classic defensive position, and they could see ... Was it? A red afro?

MOM! Felix shouted in a voice twice as loud as the one he'd used the day before. Buildings shook and trembled as his cry

echoed across the avenues of the Business District, each rever-
beration growing louder and louder, rattling Leonard's spine
and jarring his bones.

Sally reacted first.

Leonard! she shouted. Felix isn't moving!

Is that pizza I smell?

It was true. Felix was frozen solid like the dry-ice walls around
the Leader's domus.

Leonard patted his nephew's cheek, which was cold and unmoving, his mouth still pursed together forming the last momentous **M!**

In the intersection, everyone was likewise frozen; only the
horses moved about (Felix liked horses), sniffing bodies and
debris, looking for dinner, perhaps. A white spotted pony trot-
ted toward Leonard and Sally, his jouster tottering on his saddle
because his legs no longer clamped the horse's sides.

Even the eatery odors had come to a standstill.

Check Felix's health meter, Sally said, putting her collapsible-
beacon hat back on.

Leonard lifted Felix's shirt. The health meter, which should
have been slowly pulsing toward calm, wasn't moving at all!
Leonard flicked it, in case it was stuck. It wasn't.

Sally and Leonard looked at each other. They knew what this
meant. Unless and until Felix's health meter returned to normal, the world would not move, Felix would not move.

Carol! Leonard said, and rushed to his sister, who still lay curled in her defensive position. Not moving, but not frozen—unconscious. He tried to lift her from the cobbles, ruing that Pythagorean discipline had not required strength training. He gestured to Sally, who ran over to help him. Together they moved Carol twenty paces onto the side street beside Felix.

The spotted pony, who was nuzzling Felix as if to wake him, or to thank him for stopping the fighting, whinnied and shook her mane, which caused her tottering jouster to topple stiffly to the ground next to Carol, his legs now straddling air.

Now we really need a plan, said Sally, who had jumped out of the way of the jouster. But while Leonard was thinking again about how good he was at making plans, Sally said, I've got it! She tore a long slit in her orange-skin gown, then climbed onto the back of the pony, kissing and patting the pony's alabaster mane. Where there are policemen, she said, there are police caravans. Large enough to take the four of us home.

You know how to drive? Leonard asked, dumbfounded.

Of course! Sally said, and was off, headbeads bouncing, leaving Leonard in darkness once again.

The only ones licensed to drive in their town were policemen and bonded drivers of caravans, wagonettes, and liveried lorries. Police vehicles didn't even have breathreader ignitions: who would steal them? Leonard tried to imagine what the world would be like if anyone could drive—chaos, he decided. Unimaginable freedom! And Sally, already an expert! What else did he not know about this extraordinary woman?

On the ground, Carol opened her eyes.

Is that pizza I smell? And then she was out again.

Fish swimming in a sea of peasants

They managed to get Carol curled into the front seat of a police caravan. Leonard propped Felix against the side of the vehicle's holding cell, which was connected to the driver's cell by rubber voice loops, and contained a supply of yellow sashes and sniper muskets. And they were off! Sally was a very skilled driver! She didn't know Leonard's house, but she did know the caravan routes (there really was an Archive of Severely Damaged, Unreadable, Out-of-Date Caravan Directories); Leonard promised to guide her from his neighborhood stop.

So what does your Pythagorean training involve, Sally asked, if not driving and urban-survival tactics?

Well, there's Listening, and the welling of compassion, and Pythagorean meditation, and use of preapproved Listener algorithms. And receptivity, and easing of clients-in-pain. Plane geometry, of course, and tuning theory, metempsychosis and advanced soul tracing, eternal recurrence, and the spiritual qualities of the decad.

Oh, Sally said. Well, I'm sure that's good for something.

He didn't say lyre, because he'd failed lyre, and wished now he could sing Carol a Pythagorean healing song.

Leonard made Sally park at Felix's school caravan stop. He would go ahead to check heroically for nonfrozen police.

Do you have a police scanner? Sally asked, grabbing what looked like a fountain pen out of her clutchbag. When she clicked it, it shot red rays and emitted a low hum.

Leonard shook his head.

What about an ID scrambler? she asked, waving another

miniature device, which looked like a sterling needle-pusher or portable ice grinder. No? Then you had better stay here.

Leonard nodded.

Back in a tick, she said, and ran down the street, her orange-skin gown glowing in the starlight.

Leonard very much wanted to have a plan ready for her return. A good plan. For what they would do when Carol and Felix came back to life. The police would still be outside, maybe frozen, certainly ready to arrest Carol and maybe take Felix away. Where was Isaac? Why wasn't he helping?

But Sally was back and pushing a wheelbarrow.

There were six of them, she said, positioned around Carol's house, each hiding behind a tree, wearing leafy camouflage. Almost in plain sight, she said, disgusted. She hadn't needed her police scanner at all. But she did scramble the house ID: for the next long while, anyone looking at the house would be convinced he saw an abandoned caravan stop.

She wheeled Carol in the wheelbarrow, and Leonard carried Felix like firewood to the garage apartment, where they placed them gently in Leonard's bed, under warm blankets, in case that made a difference. As it happened, Leonard didn't need a plan at all: Sally had everything figured out. Under her direction, they moved the majority of Carol's clothes and other essentials out of Carol's house and into Leonard's garage apartment—specifically, under Leonard's bed. The remainder of her things they left sloppily about and forged a note: Dear Leonard and Felix, I have left our beloved land for good and taken most of my belongings with me. You must forgive me. I know you knew absolutely nothing about my activities, and were therefore entirely innocent and blameless. In fact, my own activities were innocent and blameless. Soon the police will understand this and I shall be able to come home. Leonard, Felix belongs in your conscientious care because no one else can care for his special needs as you can, and he is such a credit to our Leader. Be good to him, as I know you will. Long live the nonviolent, law-abiding Revolution!

Then they gathered emergency supplies: coin, ready edibles, string, warm hats. Sally took inflatable pockets from her clutch-bag and showed Leonard how to attach one to his belt. We need to be ready, she said.

I agree, Leonard said, but can we have dinner first?

No, Sally said. First we have to move the policemen.

With the help of the wheelbarrow, they moved the stiff, leaf-covered men to a neighbor's yard, propping them against trees that encircled a house quite like Carol's. Then for fun, they moved one or two to a house across the road.

Now we have to scramble all the house IDs, which she accomplished up and down the block. After she positioned the stolen police caravan neatly in a parkspot at the municipal compost heap, Sally agreed that, yes, it was time for dinner, but first they had to change into on-the-run clothing. Dark colors, Sally said, blend-in styles. Quiet shoes. She chose a tan house tunic and trousers from Carol's closet, and pocketed some of Carol's undergarments. For himself, Leonard chose a slim-fitting caftan and trousers that he thought showed his long legs to advantage.

Can you run in those? Sally asked. Bend? Twist? Show me.

Leonard ran a circle through the house, then, wheezing, chose a larger caftan and exchanged his open-toed clogs for some black sailing shoes.

Finally Sally agreed it was time for dinner and, no, she didn't know how to cook. So while she checked on Carol and Felix (no change), Leonard defrosted a Fish Swimming in a Sea of Peasants casserole in Carol's flash cooker and found a few scraps of haggis for Medusa, who followed Sally around as if attached to her heel by a piece of string. They ate on the settee in the no-longer-white room, with a view of Felix's drawings on the wall and the doors open, in case either Carol or Felix stirred in the other room. Neither spoke as they ate their dinner, both of them ravenous and none too dainty. When they finished, they set their bowls on the carpet and sighed and leaned back on the settee.

It was the first time they had been alone together.

Leonard wished he had some jokes to share. Look! he wanted to say, but he had nothing to show her. Why, she had more interesting things in her clutchbag than he had in his entire apartment—or his entire life.

He looked at her dumbly, all admiration and despair.

Which was when she kissed him.

Clams and sea flowers

She tasted like clams, and sea flowers. Leonard had never experienced anything so delicious, or disorienting. His heart was flummoxing, his ears let in far too much air.

Good we got that over with, Sally said, pulling away and slapping her thighs.

I'm in love with you, Leonard said, helplessly.

Yes, well, she said, we have more important things to think about.

Leonard could think of none.

Marry me, he said.

Don't be silly, she said. So what's this?

Leonard wanted to say, Your entrancing face, because that was all he could see, but Sally was pointing at the no-longer-white wall, where Felix and he had drawn pictures. Or rather, where Felix had drawn pictures—exuberant drawings of devilish monsters and eerie landscapes—while Leonard, to keep Felix company, had confined himself to a small corner behind his screen, where he drew geometric representations of the Pythagorean theorem:

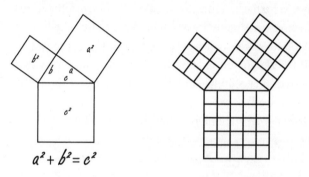

$$a^2 + b^2 = c^2$$

He'd not had much of a chance to examine Felix's drawings, which were vivid and engaging. The ugly guy over there, now that he thought about it, had to be the demon Kafkaphony with his two wives, because the two women were fighting with drawn swords—and there, in separate sandboxes, were leprous babies and babes with two heads. And that guy, standing over by the goats that looked like people, had to be Kafsephony, surrounded by infants who jumped about the ether.

Hey, Sally said, standing and looking more intently at the demon pictures, is that what I think it is?

Leonard jumped up, but he wasn't listening, for on the next wall, in front of a stand of fruit-bearing trees—the orchard of

Felix's dream, of his grandfather's stories, it had to be—blocking the view of the two Bens, the other one, and the rabbi who were about to enter, was a marvelous drawing, clearly in Felix's hand, of Leonard's grandfather! Whom Felix had never met, whom he had never even seen in a pictograph. The figure was waving his arms, madly.

As in, literally: his arms were moving, right there on the no-longer-white wall; he was trying to get Leonard's attention!

Grandfather! Leonard shouted. Isaac! Talk to me! How do we get Felix back? How do we keep Carol from the police?

Leonard? What is it? Are you okay? Sally asked.

Don't you see? Leonard asked, pointing at the wall.

Boychik, she don't see it.

You don't see it! he said. It's Isaac, he's waving. He's talking! From the wall!

Don't worry about her, boychik. I need you to listen good. You did very very good with the Baconians.

Sally tugged on Leonard's caftan. Who's Isaac? The new Chief Librarian? Is this one of your tricks?

Shh, Leonard whispered. Go check Felix. I'll tell you later.

She left the room, reluctantly, looking at Leonard over her shoulder.

Felix is okay, boychik, but you have to get him, I am sorry for this. There is no other way.

Get him? Now?

Leonard turned to leave the room and saw the shadow of Sally, hiding behind the door.

No, boychik. I don't mean from the other room, I mean from the other century.

We're listening

Boychik, I need you to listen good. Felix is with a very good, very important man. This man is taking care of him, but I need you to bring him home.

An important man? Another century? What is he doing there? Where is Felix!

Listen, you don't know this man. He is Abulafia.

Abulafia? Spanish mystic? Worked with Hebrew letters?

Yes, I forget. The girl.

Abulafia? said Sally from behind the door.

Isaac! What is Felix doing in the thirteenth century! Where is he?!

Not to worry about it. I had to send him, or his brain explode. He is too young for this, boychik. Nothing for it. He need Abulafia to control his powers. Very simple.

Sally and Felix have Abulafianism, Leonard said.

Abulafia? Sally said from behind the door.

Silly phrase, but yes, they share this Special Gift.

Sally thinks she's lost it. She's very sad.

Not lost, never lost. You fix the Voynich, you did good, this is very very necessary. Now I need you to listen good. Boychik!

But Leonard was behind the door, hugging Sally.

Everything's okay, he said. You still have your Special Gift. Felix is with Abulafia, we're going to get him!

Abulafia is dead!

Isaac knows what he's doing.

Boychik!

WHO'S ISAAC?

Leonard led Sally by the hand back to the no-longer-white room.

Sally, meet Isaac; Isaac, Sally.

Yes yes, Isaac said. I need you to listen, Lenny.

Where is he? Sally said.

We're listening, Leonard said.

Finally! Isaac said. So this is how it goes.

Stop kissing the girl

Isaac explained to Leonard, and Leonard to Sally: Carol and Felix would be safe in Leonard's garage apartment until they returned; they would find and know Abulafia by unmistakable signs. Most important, to save Felix, they had to convince Abulafia *not to meet Pope Nicholas till Rosh Hashanah*—later was okay, but any earlier and Felix, and they for that matter, would remain in the thirteenth century forever. The current world, then, the world they knew and loved, would stay frozen until the End of Days. Only there would be no End of Days, because there would be no Messiah to bring on the End of Days, heaven forbid!

Repeat after me, Isaac said.

He wants us to repeat after him.

I can't hear him.

You repeat after me, buttercup.

Repeat after me, Isaac said. What do you convince Abulafia of?

What do you convince Abulafia of?

What do you convince Abulafia of?

No! You are not listening!

Isaac! We are listening!

Isaac! We are listening!

Start over, Isaac said. You are such a literal boy. Answer my question: What must you do to save Felix and unfreeze the world?

We must convince Abulafia not to visit Pope Nicholas until Rosh Hashanah!

We must convince Abulafia not to visit Pope Nicholas until Rosh Hashanah!

You know what is the Rosh Hashanah, boychik?

No.

No.

We're not repeating anymore, Leonard whispered to Sally, and then, because he couldn't help it, he kissed her muddled forehead.

Birthday of the world, boychik. You explain this later. She will come up with the explanation that will convince Abulafia, you trust her.

Leonard kissed Sally's forehead again.

You're going to save us, he whispered. You're going to figure it all out!

Sally looked very pleased with herself.

You trust her with this one thing, Isaac said, but you don't tell her anything what we do. The time will come. She will choose her destiny, then she can know anything. Not till then.

Leonard nodded and turned to Sally. You will choose your destiny, he said. Then you can know everything.

So what will happen, boychik, if you do not do as I say?

If we don't do as you say, we will be stuck in the thirteenth century forever and the world will never unfreeze.

Sally gasped.

Not till the End of Days, Isaac said. Only there won't be an End of Days.

Not till the End of Days, Leonard said. Only there won't be an End of Days.

So stop kissing the girl, boychik, and listen.

PART THREE
THE SIZZLING ALEPH

Can't do better

Can't do better, a man was saying.

They were standing on wet cobblestones on a dark, narrow street, conversing with a man who wore a yellow straw hat over his pageboy haircut, and a knee-length tunic over a linen shirt and hose. On his feet were soft leather slippers that looked like they'd been turned inside out. His fingernails were indescribably dirty and he smelled like fish.

Where had Isaac landed them? The thirteenth century, presumably, but where?

No decent establishment will take ye on spec, the man added. Go elsewhere and ye'll have to share yer chamber with indigent Frisians and Franks. Whereas I am willing to wait till ye locate florins amongst yer alleged relations here.

Leonard nodded, abstractly, trying to catch up with the conversation, which seemed to have started without him. It had rained recently; the air was steamy with moisture and already sweat was accumulating on Leonard's forehead and back. How wise Sally had been to insist he replace his slim-fitting caftan and trousers!

Who is this, then? the man asked, pointing at Sally. Yer wife?

Sister, Leonard said, just as Sally said, Wife.

'Tis Abraham and Sarah, 'tis it? the man said, laughing at his own inexplicable wit. Not to worry, this is no uncivilized land where a man must call his wife sister to save himself from murder. No one is opportuned or misabused in my hostellery!

Though I fully admit yer caution, I do, and there are other hostelleries—all of them, in fact—where'd ye'd be not so keenly looked after. Have we decided, then? Shall we go up? What has happened to yer staffs, by the bye, were they stolen along with yer scrips and yer baldrics?

Leonard did not know how to answer that.

A cat's blink

Their voyage hadn't been what you'd expect. There was no whirring "time tumbler" or kaleidoscopic sinkhole. There was just a circle, a mixing of letters in Sally's head, a silent singing by Leonard of the clapping song, some general hopping and dancing, according to a well-established pattern, and a mysterious extra ingredient offered by Isaac, which Sally and Leonard could neither see nor hear.

It was over in a flash of light, yet it took an entire lifetime. As Leonard hurtled, motionless, through a still yet throbbing conglomeration of space and time, he became reacquainted with his most important moments. Banging a lollisucker on his babycage as a tall be-afroed man approached and said, Let's see those little teeth, Lenny, they're bothering you again, ain't they?

His father? He might have cried to remember this, had he either eyes or time. His grandfather was there, younger than Leonard remembered, and dancing—yes, dancing—in the candlelight. Oy, he was singing, Oy, oy, oy! Yet he looked happy—because there, dancing with him, holding his hands and lifting her knees, was a redheaded woman who looked rather like Carol, only happy. Leonard's mother? His mother? Leonard's age, as he was now, dancing in joy. Little Lenny toddling over, breaking into the circle so he might dance as well.

His grandfather's face, older now, bearing the news that would make Lenny hide amid his grandfather's books, staining the leather with his orphan's tears. And Carol, barely eighteen, saying, How can I take care of an old man and a little boy? Crying to Joseph, her boyfriend, when they couldn't hear—Joseph, who was there, and then not, his oboe and music stand suddenly gone, Carol's clarinet thrown now into the compost-masher—no time for that, she said, her face puffy, her expression hard. Leonard had forgotten about the boyfriend, he'd forgotten about the clarinet.

There was more: old book smell and helping his grandfather to the toilet, the angry feeling in his chest when he called the old man stupid, his stories and books and herring jokes stupid, his grandfather's eyes slipping from blue to palest green, his grandfather calling him boychik and reminding him to tell his stories only to his grandsons. Awaking in a place as empty as the Desert of Lop when his grandfather died, then the birth two years later of Felix, like a second chance. All these memories and images swirled simultaneously and instantaneously, in less time than it would take for a cat to blink: and when Leonard opened his eyes, they were there.

Feet like oranges

Ye'll be wanting pottage and ale, I expect, the man continued, leading them up an exterior staircase to the second floor of his hostellery.

Leonard didn't know what pottage was but couldn't imagine anything less appealing than dining at this establishment, unless it was the building itself, which smelled of damp, barnyard animals, and human effluence.

Yes, please, he said.

My Froga is standing o'er the blandreth now, a'stirrin' and a'mixin'. But mebbe they don't eat such where ye come from? Yer dressed so strange, whence is it ye hail? My pilgrims come from every part of this flat earth but I've never seen footing quite so, well, ye don't mind me saying, quite so strange as yers.

He was referring to Leonard's sailing shoes, with their whisper-quiet ground-suckers.

We are from Cathay, Leonard said, surprising himself. I assure you that in that land our clothes are of the highest fashion. Only the richest merchants and princes of the highest rank wear clothing such as ours.

Ah, the man said. Well, then. And what exactly do ye merchant, if I may ask?

Cathay noodles, Leonard said, then wished he hadn't.

Not a product that has made its mark hereabouts, the hosteller observed.

Not yet, Leonard said grandly. Now I'll thank you to forget I ever mentioned it.

I haven't much of a memory for things I ain't seen. So where be yer Cathay?

Well beyond the Levant, Leonard essayed, and full of wonders. You'll be reading about it soon enough. We have all manner of custom unbeknownst to you. Our ladies' feet are bound when young till they are the size and shape of oranges—we find it most becoming. We drink elegant infusions of sticks and grass. Plus, we have a wall that extends hundreds of versts around our land.

This lady's feet seem well larger than an orange, the man mused.

I told you already, Leonard said. She is the wife of a rich merchant. She doesn't need feet like oranges.

I take yer point, then, the man said, but none the less, ye must know the lady's outfit is, well, scandalizing. Pilgrim or no, merchant or no, she will be mobbed and defrocked, such will be the people's outrage. I say this because 'tis my Christian duty to prevent violence and rapine. Yer Christians, I suspect? Ye'd have no cause to pilgrim were ye not.

In a manner of speaking, Leonard said, not quite ready to enter into theological debate.

Whatever heresy ye partake of, ye'll need some pilgrim gear, if yer to travel about as romei.

Romei?

Pilgrims who come to Rome.

So they were in Rome, Leonard thought.

Have ye ought to trade for yer lodgings, perhaps in the lady's scrip?

He was ogling Sally's clutchbag. He apparently hadn't noticed the inflatable pocket under Leonard's tunic.

I note it was not taken from ye with yer other belongings on that dangerous route to Rome. I also note it is of uncommon size.

I assure you . . . , Leonard said.

Or perhaps that rare bit about yer wrist?

He was referring to Leonard's navigator watch.

Sally spoke for the first time: We'll exchange that rare piece of jewelry for thirty days' stay in your fine hostellery. And porridge and ale for all that time ...

We do have other victuals! the man protested.

And other victuals, Sally agreed, and clean clothing appropriate for romei.

Sally! Leonard protested. Carol gave me this watch!

And she'll give you another when we bring Felix home, she whispered.

It is motioned by angels, Leonard said. Look! and he removed the watch so the innkeeper could see the second-counter pulsing.

Motioned by angels, the man murmured. Ye shall have yer exchange, and then some, for I am an honest man. Whom ye might call Bobolo, for such is my name. Bobolo Savelli, no relation.

With that puzzling aside, Bobolo showed them to their room.

Amazing!

You were amazing out there, Sally said.

I was? Leonard said.

Cathay? Infusion of sticks? Who knew you had such an imagination!

Rather than credit Milione, Leonard said, No, you were amazing! Trading the navigator watch like that!

I want Dwane to trace that guy thinking he's us!

They smiled at each other in mutual amazement, then, embarrassed, looked about the room.

Bobolo had pointed out the fine straw mattress, a mere generation old, and the chamberpot, which he'd called a jordan, explaining, again mysteriously, that he hadn't an outside necessarium with which to receive their exalted wastage. He'd taken time, too, to show them the back garden, where piebald dogs rooted through an uncontained compost heap, and also the dining chamber. Leonard had wanted to examine the bedclothes—he suspected they were none too clean—but was violently struck by the fact that it was a bed, and he and Sally were expected to share it.

Don't go near that, Sally said. It's covered with fleas—I can see them jumping from here. I have snugbeds in here somewhere—and she upended her clutchbag onto the rough planked floor, and out fell numerous objects, some of which Leonard recognized, including Sally's police scanner. There, she said, handing Leonard a square of microsilk. The plaid one's for you, the red one's for me. Push the button so—and up puffed a single-unit snugbed complete with micropillow.

There was a knock. Leonard opened the door a crack.

Where we come from, Leonard said, only peasants sleep on beds. We are only slightly insulted but we will need you to take this noxious bedding away.

Behind him, Leonard could hear the sound of snugbeds deflating.

Ascetics, Bobolo said approvingly. My best customers!

Oh, Leonard said, not knowing what Bobolo meant.

Here's yer pilgrims' gear, Bobolo said, trying to see around Leonard. The wearers did not die of any contamination, just yer normal afflictions, no fear.

Ah, Leonard said, taking the gear through the sliver of doorway.

The scallop means ye've been to Compostela, in case ye didn't know.

We knew that, Leonard said. Why would you think we wouldn't know that? and he closed the door.

The scallop Bobolo referred to was a tin seashell pinned to the wide, upfolded brims of their new hats. The clothes, rough woven, consisted of sleeved tunics, mantles, hose, and simple leather shoes in well-worn brown and black—Sally was to wear the same as Leonard, apparently. Accoutrements included a leather pouch for each affixed to a leather strap that was to cross their chest—scrips and baldrics, presumably. Also, plain wooden walking staffs with knobs at one end.

The two turned their backs so they could dress.

Notice anything funny about the way that man talks? Sally asked. No! Don't turn around!

Well, Leonard said, blushing (because she'd seen that he'd been about to turn), his language was a bit odd.

No, silly. I mean that we understand him. Shouldn't he be speaking Italian or Latin or something?

It's Isaac, he said. He translates, in his own way.

Don't you think it's time you told me what's going on?

Sally was right. Asking no questions, she'd traveled to this strange place and time, with no assurance that she'd ever return, and why? To rescue a boy she barely knew. Well, maybe she also wanted to meet Abulafia and get her powers back.

Leonard opened his mouth to explain, or rather, he half opened his mouth, or rather he was about to open his mouth, when the room began to shake and he was flung most urgently to the ground.

Okay, Sally said, her face white. I guess it can wait.

Just like Augustine

What time do you think it is? Leonard asked, after he'd dusted himself off.

Sally looked out the window. Judging from the position of the sun, I'd say midday. Twelve or one. Give or take. Depending on the time of year. And the weather. And our longitude and latitude.

Leonard resolved never to be amazed by Sally again. To be amazed by her amazingness was a betrayal, an indication that he didn't think her always amazing.

Sally opened their door and listened.

There are people downstairs, Sally said. Let's see what they know.

Can I kiss you first? Leonard asked.

Intelligence first, kiss later.

Downstairs, milling about, were pilgrims from every corner of the world. Lombards and Cumbrians, Russians too. An old English lady was describing, with much awe, the grill that roasted Saint Lawrence, while a spindly Hungarian described the stone that had hurtled the martyr Abundus to his sewery death. A sprightly Sicilian explained to a phlegmatic Croat that he'd visited the vernicle of Veronica twice, and received eighteen thousand years of indulgence for his sins. Several discussed the horrors of their journey. A redheaded Swabian described a narrow escape from a monster two cubits long—with a carmine cat's head, the legs of a fish, the bifid tongue of a snake, and a hairy trailing tail! Another described having survived two avalanches, a flooded river, and an outsize case of vertigo.

There was little to distinguish the pilgrims' dress, but they did wear a variety of badges—the Compostela scallop shell, also tiny keys, a medallion of a woman holding a cloth on which was imprinted the image of a man's suffering face. Some badges were pinned, some sewn onto hats, others hung about the neck.

Greetings! Leonard said to a Frankish pair. How's the pilgrimming?

We have been to three of the four patriarchal basilicas! the husband exclaimed. Tonight we go to St. Peter's!

The wife nodded a gentle Frankish nod.

Do you know Abulafia? Sally said.

The pair shook their heads, puzzled—and why not? Leonard realized. Foreigners, here to see the holy sites of Christendom—what would they know of a Jewish mystic from Spain?

You are from? the Frankish wife asked.

Cathay, Leonard said.

Their eyes opened wide.

Beyond the Levant, Leonard said proudly. We're Manicheans—and immediately the room hushed. He had no idea what Manicheans were, only that they hailed from Cathay.

You are heretics? the husband whispered.

Ex-Manicheans! Sally said loudly. Like Augustine.

Ah, the man said, relieved. Like Augustine!

Like Augustine! Leonard said, having no notion who Augustine was.

Not heretics! the Frankish woman said.

Not heretics at all, the Frankish man agreed.

So where are the Jews? Sally said.

Again, that strange look.

We wish to convert them, Sally explained, and again their Frankish faces cleared.

No idea, the Frankish man said, and no one seemed to know what to say.

Nice baldrick! Leonard said to the man. Nice scrip! he said to the wife.

The Frankish pair looked to each other for guidance.

Boy, am I ready for victuals! Leonard said.

The Franks smiled—they too!

Hey, look, there's pottage!

Midday victuals, arranged on a long wooden table surrounded by low benches, consisted of a slimy water-thing (eel, according to Sally) and a sloppy stewy thing, which someone, with apparent approval, referred to as *pottage* (as in *Hey, look, there's pottage!*). Ale was served in glasses that, apparently, were to be shared, and the food was served not on plates but on large pieces of heavy brown bread.

To communicate with the serving wench, the Frankish couple referred to a small book, from which they retrieved useful phrases such as Is this eel quite fresh? And I believe this eel to be not quite fresh. And Perhaps I can parley with the manager?

You got food in your clutchbag? Leonard whispered.

For emergencies, she whispered back. We're already too conspicuous, thanks to you!

Me! Leonard whispered back. You could have been a bit more discreet!

Me! Sally said, almost in full voice. You told everyone we were heretics!

The two might have continued had there not come from the

front of the building a bone-shattering, heart-quaking shriek—a shriek so loud and momentous that had Felix screamed thus, the earth and heavens, and time and space besides, would have frozen for all eternity.

The men jumped to their feet, Leonard among them; the Frankish woman began to cry. Before anyone could investigate, a scraggly servant in a knee-length tunic arrived panting at the door. Be not afeard! he said. Everything is absolutely, perfectly fine, it is dandy, A-one, and absolutely right as rain—though he hardly seemed to believe it, ashen as he was.

He smiled and ambled over to Leonard, more quickly than casually.

Would ye be Messer Leonard? he then asked softly in his ear. I was told to look for the man with the ebullient hair.

Leonard nodded.

Would ye be so kind, Messer Leonard, as to come with me? he asked. Superfast, sir, as in right now?

The rest of the pilgrims, satisfied that all was well, asked that the pottage be passed.

The devil within

Though not invited, Sally followed Leonard into a small room a few paces from the hostellery's entryway. There the innkeeper lay limply on a couch, his face yellow, his pageboy hair clammy and stuck to his forehead. A woman wearing a pillbox hat secured to her head by a white chin strap was massaging Bobo-lo's large, naked feet. She seemed unbothered by their stench, which quite overpowered the smell of pottage. Squeezed in the hosteller's hand was Leonard's navigator watch.

What is this devilry ye have sold me? he gasped. Ye said it were motioned by angels.

So it is! Leonard said.

A devil resides within!

Leonard stooped to take the watch from Bobolo's hand.

The innkeeper had somehow managed to summon the Brazen Head. It was sitting atop a golden throne, wearing a tinfoil crown and eating jujuberries. It was excessively fat today, and shirtless. Every few moments it spat a jujuberry, which bounced off the bald head of a dejected jester. The Head was smirking, no doubt about it.

Without thinking, Leonard pressed the Speak to Me button on the watch's underside.

We don't need you, he said to the Head. Go away.

Which meant the Brazen Head was free to speak. His voice was high-pitched and louder than you might think:

Where are you, Leonard! We're going to find you! It doesn't matter where you are, we'll find you!

Leonard pressed the Go to Sleep button, but not before Bobolo fell to the floor in a faint.

Damned pilgrims, the woman muttered, and set about reviving Bobolo with vigorous slaps. It took their combined strength to get him back onto the couch. The young servant, shaking, was sent to fetch brandy—for the wife, not the husband, whose soul eventually rejoined them with groans, sighs, and a series of voiceless bilabial plosives: Pah ... pah ... pah!

What is it, husband? the wife asked, kneeling by his side. Do ye wish an audience with yer father confessor? Do ye wish to apologize to yer wife for dying a poor man, and a puttock besides?

Weakly, the man pushed his wife's face away.

Leave me, wagtail! Return to yer coven. I'll not be needing anything from ye.

The wife squinted at Leonard and Sally, then left the room, her skirt swishing against the floor. Bobolo reached for Leonard's hand. From the strength of the man's grip, Leonard judged he would make it.

I do not wish devils in my home, he whispered.

No, no, Leonard said, kneeling down. This is no devil. I swear it.

The innkeeper raised himself weakly onto an elbow.

Is it perchance a soul awaiting judgment? he whispered. Does this reliquary offer a portal to Purgatory?

There is wisdom within, Leonard said, reckoning that this was true enough.

It mentioned yer name, the man whispered, collapsing back onto the divan. It seemed angry.

It wasn't happy that I'd gifted it to you. I had to explain that I was no longer its master.

Master? Do I hold power over that small anguished soul?

Leonard looked to Sally for assistance.

We can put it in its place, she said. But first you must tell us: What day is it?

Jew magic

Bobolo, empowered by curiosity, uprighted himself.

What day is it? Is she mad? he whispered to Leonard.

Very much not so, Leonard assured him, though he had no idea what Sally was thinking.

The date, please.

The hosteller gave her a date in late August, year of our Lord 1280.

And when is the birthday of the world?

Bobolo looked crestfallen.

Is this a riddle? Because I am not so clever with riddles, Froga can tell ye.

Where is Pope Nicholas? How does one go about consulting him?

Ye wish to consult the pope?

No, Sally said. We want to consult a Jewish sage—and finally Leonard understood: Sally wanted them to get on with their business. Where would they find Abulafia, and how much time did they have before he had to visit the pope?

Is there Jew magic in this here reliquary? the innkeeper asked. I thought mebbe so.

Not at all, Leonard assured him.

Well, yer Jewish sage should be knocking any minute, Bobolo said, or I don't know my Froga.

Bobolo did know his wife, Froga, for in with Froga walked a black-hatted, gray-bearded gentleman, who demanded that Bobolo lie down for pity's sake. A circular yellow badge was sewn to his tunic.

Zedekiah Anaw, Bobolo said by way of introduction. Jew physician. I have very nearly died, he explained, on account of this little devil person here, which may or may not be the result of Jew magic. Can ye tell? In this reliquary here. He's meant to be strapped to my wrist, but truly I am afeard.

The man applied his palm to the innkeeper's forehead.

Thou ravest yet thou art not feverish! the man marveled.

Again with Isaac's translation!

I assure ye, my mind is as clear as the Tiber! Bobolo protested.

Then 'tis none too clear! Zedekiah replied.

These here're Manicheans from Cathay, Bobolo said. They sold me the demon for some pilgrims' fare.

A quick look at Leonard and Sally confirmed Zedekiah's diagnosis.

I would wish thou didst not excite thyself. Prithee, withhold thy speech until the morrow.

Perhaps he wants fleeming? Froga asked hopefully.

I do not put stock in bleeding, Mistress Froga, as well thou knowest.

He put his hand to Bobolo's wrist, then to his chest.

Thy heart doth gallop. Mistress Froga, he said, standing now, I shall send to thee a boy with herbs. Thou shalt make of them a hearty infusion, according to instructions I shall give thee. If the raving increaseth, or if thou noticest a burning or ague, thou shouldst sendeth for me without delay.

I'm not raving, damn ye! Bobolo said.

Shh! Froga replied. Of course ye are.

When is the birthday of the world? Sally asked the healer.

Zedekiah considered Sally for a moment and half smiled.

What dost a Manichean from Cathay care for the birthday of the world?

We are looking for Abraham Abulafia. Do you know him?

Zedekiah Anaw was no longer amused.

This man of whom thou speakest doth not exist. His name and mystic activity are but a rumor intended to bring disrepute to our small community. Thou wouldst do well to return to Cathay, if this is thy suit. Good day, he said, and made to leave.

Isaac the Blind sent us, Leonard said before the man could reach the door.

Zedekiah stopped short and looked back.

What sayest thou?

My nephew is missing. His name is Felix. Isaac sent us to find him.

Zedekiah looked at the pair another long moment.

The birthday of the world is in six days' time, he said, and again he smiled that half smile. If the boy thou seekest is Asher, thou shalt find him by answering this: What is purple, hangs on the wall, and whistles?

Whistles? Leonard said, his face ashen. Hangs on the wall?

Thy good friend Isaac canst perhaps aid thee with the deciphering. Though he be dead some forty years, I am sure he shall oblige thee. Good day.

Felix is not in the river!

Leonard watched, unmoving, as Zedekiah "bade them adieu." Sally had to grab his arm and pull him to the dining hall. The pilgrims were gone and all that remained of the victuals was some crusted pottage and a few slimy fish things.

I know the answer, Leonard said.

You do not, Sally said.

It's herring, Leonard replied. It is.

It can't be, Sally said. Herring isn't purple.

It is if you paint it purple.

But it doesn't hang on the wall!

It does if you hang it on the wall.

This is a dumb riddle. It doesn't make sense.

It isn't a riddle, it's a joke pretending to be a riddle.

Herrings don't whistle!

Okay, so it doesn't whistle—that's the punch line. It's a herring joke, an old Jewish joke that makes no sense. My grandfather used to tell it. But I don't know what it means. How can herring help us find Felix?

We'll find Felix where there are fish!

Leonard looked at his beloved with all possible admiration.

You think so? he asked.

Definitely! We look for Felix where they catch fish, where they sell fish, where they eat fish.

Sally smiled, content with herself.

He doesn't mean in the river?

Sally and Leonard looked at each other, stricken.

No, Sally decided. That's not what he meant. Felix is not in the river.

Right, Leonard agreed. Felix is not in the river. Felix is definitely not in the river!

Dreams of revolutionary stew

It was early afternoon when Leonard lay down in his snugbed— it was still his habit to sleep days, and he was muddled about whether it was day or night, given that he'd traveled more than seven centuries and had relived his entire lifetime. He'd rest just a moment, he told Sally, and then they could decide where to find fish. Sally didn't know whether to be angry or amused.

He awoke sometime later to the sound of Sally's voice at the foot of the stairs.

We'd like to make a study of your fishing industry, he heard her say. We are fisherpeople in Cathay.

I thought ye were noble folk, Bobolo replied, equally loudly, recovered from his fit, apparently.

We are noble folk, Sally said, as if exercising great patience. Our people are noble fisherpeople.

Ye'll want to go to the river, then. Where else would ye go?

And which direction is that?

Straight, Bobolo said. But ye'll not get yer indulgences there. Fer them, ye've got to visit the churches.

Fish first, churches later, Sally said.

He awoke somewhat later to the sound of fierce rains. Something told him that the locals would not respond well to the rainshields Sally had packed in his inflatable pocket—the sound of their miniature engines, he imagined, would cause many to faint. They would have to rely on their pilgrims' hats and cloaks.

Then he was dreaming—of revolutionary stew. It was everything Carol said it was! Succulent and nutritious, plump and steaming. He decided in his dream that when he awoke, he'd suggest Revolutionary Stew Pizza to his employers, Neetsa Pizza! But Sally—dear Sally! beloved Sally!—was shoving his shoulder.

Get up! she said. Hurry!

Unthinking, Leonard pulled her to him—she would share his stew, what was his was hers, for now and ever more, even if it was made into pizza! Especially if it was made into pizza! But instead of enjoying the stew, she slapped his face—hard!—and pulled his afro till his eyes teared.

Get up! We've gotta get out of here! NOW!

Leonard became dimly aware of a hullabaloo downstairs, the sound of shouting and protesting in at least three Isaac-induced speaking styles. Sally yanked on Leonard's arm, pulling at him to get him out of his snugbed. She was still fully dressed, her face exasperated.

Now! she said. UP!

Leonard blinked, looked around, tried to recall where he was.

She dropped Leonard's clothes on his face, his inflatable pocket too; she might have been ready to cry.

We have to RUN! she cried, Come on! and was in the hallway, from which Leonard could hear—more distinctly now that the door was open—Bobolo's wheedling voice:

It weren't me put the little fella in the reliquary! It were the Manicheans!

Froga added stridently: We was only performing a service, yer honor, demonstulating what befalls the wicked in Purgatory, like!

These words awakened Leonard entirely, but it takes time to get out of a snugbed: the microsilk, once inflated, conforms to the body's shape, holding it, well, snugly for optimal sleep. Egress requires considerable wriggling if one lacks time for full deflation, which Leonard decidedly lacked, as he could hear a deep masculine voice downstairs exclaiming, WHERE BE THE MISCREANTS WHO HATH SOLD THEE THIS DEVIL'S PLAYTHING? I SHOULD LIKE TO HARM THEM—FOR EXAMPLE, WITH A **HEAD VISE!**

That's right! Bobolo said. Ye don't want to harm us, yer very highest Inquisitorial honor. It's them ye want! A head vise'll do it! They're right up the stairs there, second door to yer left.

Right, Froga said.

Right, Bobolo amended.

Left, ye puttock! Froga said.

Left, right, said Bobolo.

Leonard had squiggled his entire top half from his snugbed, but his legs remained, and they were quite long. He could hear heavy boots begin to clomp ploddingly across the common area downstairs.

THE HEATHENS BE UP HERE? the deep-voiced man thundered from the bottom of the stairs.

Yep, yer honor—Froga's voice again. I always said these people was strange.

At last Leonard had squeezed his feet from the snugbed.

I SHOULD LIKE TO MEET THESE STRANGE PEOPLE! exclaimed the man with the deep voice. I SHOULD LIKE TO FLAY THEM—FOR EXAMPLE, WITH A **SCRAMASAX**!

Leonard stumbled out of the room, holding tight to his pilgrims' gear but dropping his inflatable pocket. He was surprised to see flashing red lights at one end of the hall.

This way! Sally hissed from the other end of the hall as heavy boots began plonking up the steps. PUM! ... PUM! ... PUM!

Run! Sally whisper-shouted. And Leonard did—away from the stairs and down the windowless hallway, barefoot, wearing only his crayon-colored sleeping togs, his heart pounding, his health meter thrumming, to the outer staircase, where Sally, dear, blessed, ever vigilant Sally, held open the door.

A familiar face

She'd left her police scanner behind, to distract their pursuers with its shooting red rays and low-level hum. As Leonard flew through the door to the outer stairwell, he heard the man, newly arrived upon the landing, say, WHAT IS THIS? A FIRE THAT DOTH NOT CONSUME? STAND BACK! WE ARE WITNESS TO A MIRACLE! DO NOT LOOK UPON IT! NO ONE SHALL LOOK UPON IT AND LIVE!

What happened? Leonard asked as they paused at the bottom of the external staircase, on the narrow cobblestoned street outside the hostellery. It was dusk, but they could still see a large group of pilgrims confrering by the hostellery door.

No time, Sally said, and they were running again.

Leonard was barely able to note his surroundings—which consisted chiefly of crumbling two-story buildings, and assorted bundle-bearing women who observed his sleeping togs with shock and amusement—but he did, as they raced headlong down the road, notice, peeping out from an alleyway, a familiar face, belonging to a man with a beard, a hat, and a yellow circle on his cloak.

Running and stopping

They ran in a zigzag pattern, Leonard following Sally in and out of dark alleyways, turning right, past towers and perfumed churches, and left, past fluted columns embedded between thick brick arches, and right, past wells and gardens and little houses and fly-ridden butcher shops, then left, past more churches, and strange ruined buildings, tiny bread shops, and spice shops, and fabric shops, all closing now (with loud cries from their owners of last-minute bargains), dodging horse dung and cow patties and other excretions, bumping into urchins and bawdy girls and sending street cats screeching and flying.

They didn't hear their pursuer's heavy boots behind them, but still they ran.

Till Leonard could run no farther.

Enough! he gasped, and pointed at the portico of a church. Sally doubled back, and they climbed two stairs into the portico and rested their backs against a marble column. It was fully evening now, but still warm.

You need to get your clothes on, Sally said after Leonard had stopped panting.

Thank you, Leonard said.

No need to be sarcastic! Sally said.

I mean, thank you. You saved me! You could have left me behind but you didn't.

And be stuck in this wretched place forever?

Leonard looked around. They were in the narrowest possible lane. Too narrow for a police caravan, or even for two to walk hand in hand. But there was something warm in the brick of the house across the lane, with its ancient well and garden visible in back, something lovely too about the fluted columns in front of this church—older than the church itself, he guessed. Something comforting about the dusky summer air and the sound, if one listened hard, of at least two babies crying.

It's not so bad, he said.

You're wrong, Sally said.

Leonard shrugged.

Did you see Zedekiah? He was outside the inn, watching.

You sure? Sally said. I don't think so.

Leonard shrugged again, then told Sally to look away as he went behind a column to change into his pilgrim's clothes. She sat down on a marble step, her toe tracing the cobblestones.

I dropped my inflatable pocket, Leonard said from behind the column.

Oh, great! Sally said. There goes our supply of grasshopper legs, and your change of clothes, and my string and hold-alls.

I didn't mean to drop it, Leonard said.

But you did, Sally replied.

Yes, Leonard agreed, I did.

Now what're we going to do?

Leonard didn't know. The loss of Sally's string didn't seem a terrible thing—compared with flaying, say, or having one's head clamped in a vise—but maybe that's not what she meant. He joined her on the marble step.

What happened back there? he asked. At the inn? Why all the commotion?

Bobolo was charging coins to see the miracle of the navigator watch. Pilgrims were queuing down the road—you saw them, right? I guess someone decided it was dangerous.

Ah, Leonard said.

It was rapidly darkening, and quiet now, the street empty.

I let you down, Sally said.

What?

It was my idea to give Bobolo the navigator watch. I thought it was funny. I almost got us killed.

No way! It was a great idea!

Yeah? We're missing half our stuff, we have no lucre, we're in the middle of a city we don't know, following a riddle we're not sure we understand.

Leonard took her hand.

We'll figure it out. We won't let Felix down. We'll find the river. We'll find Felix.

And if we find a river? What then? Sally said to her leather slippers. How will that help us find Felix?

Leonard pondered that. Pythagoras had once addressed a river, which spoke back to him: Hail, Pythagoras! it said. But Leonard was no Pythagoras, nor would Hail, Leonard! help them much.

Isaac said to look for signs, he said. We'll look for signs.

I'm not so good at that.

Sure you are! You understood that we were in danger, right?

Where are we going to sleep tonight, Leonard? This place gives me the creeps.

We'll find something. Don't worry. How about we eat something?

Sally rummaged in her clutchbag.

All we have is some bridies and a few ham stix, she said.

We'd better wait, then, Leonard said.

It's almost night. Where are we supposed to go?

Leonard didn't want to worry Sally, but in his view, a lack of food, coin, lodging, and friends was the least of their worries: there was also the man with the boots.

We need to be somewhere where we won't be conspicuous, Leonard said. A crowded place, where we won't be noticed.

Can you ask your friend Isaac for help?

He doesn't come when I call, Leonard said. He likes to surprise me.

There must be something you can do!

Leonard thought about how Isaac had contacted him in the past: on the telephone, in a dream, prancing on Leonard's wall or screen. He wouldn't speak unless or until he was sure Leonard was paying attention. Then he berated him for not listening properly.

I have to listen, Leonard said. That's what I have to do.

Signs and wonders

I'll start by practicing *echemythia*, Leonard said, Pythagorean meditation. It won't take but a minute, and he scooched up a step or two till he was sitting on the portico floor, his legs pretzeled, his eyes closed. He began by imagining he was wearing white in a White Room; he took a deep breath, then another. And ignored, or tried to ignore, the mosquito on his neck, then twisted his neck a bit, to get rid of the mosquito, then slapped it, then slipped into silence. Deep silence, Pythagorean silence, except for the sound of some Franks, a man and a woman, approaching along the cobblestoned road.

They were evil, the woman was saying.

I'm not sure that they were, the man said.

I tell you, they were evil. With their heresies and strange questions.

A problem with translation, I'm sure.

They were walking straight past Leonard and Sally but in the darkness did not see them.

Are we going the right way?

Absolutely, the man said.

That eel was not quite fresh, the Frankish woman said.

We can change hostelleries tomorrow, the man said.

It's awfully quiet, dearest. They said St. Peter's was busy and loud, with all the dirty pilgrims sleeping there.

It is but minutes away. Cross the bridge and left at the fortress. I am told we cannot miss it.

You have no idea where we are.

You can smell the censers from here, my love.

Their voices faded. Sally pinched Leonard's thigh.

Did you hear that? she whispered.

I was trying not to, Leonard whispered back, opening his eyes and shifting out of his pretzel, to the great relief of his knees.

It was a sign! Sally said. Bridge, river, crowded place where pilgrims sleep: they told us where to go!

Excellent! Leonard said, though he wasn't sure of that, he wasn't sure at all.

The torches of a thousand pilgrims

They gathered their few belongings and began walking down the lane, looking for a bridge to a fortress. The darkness was absolute, as there was no street lighting, no Hello! lamps on Everything's-Okay poles anywhere.

Do you have your personal beta-version collapsible beacon?

You mean, the hat I designed based on Baconian optics?

You designed that?

Of course!

Yes, I mean that collapsible beacon.

Gone, Sally said. Maybe I left it at the hostellery.

Leonard smiled: it wasn't only he who had left things behind.

That's alright, he said. He would have taken her hand had the road been wide enough.

Look! he said, and pointed—at more stars than either had ever seen in a sky.

Nice, Sally said, without enthusiasm.

There's the Neetsa Pizza logo. See? The triangle with the pepperoni? Next to the Heraclitan flame?

Sally nodded.

Ironic, considering how the Heraclitans hate us—Oh! he said, lifting his nose into the air. Can you smell that?

I smell compost—and in fact, they'd passed a vacant lot teeming with mounds of it.

No, it's something else.

What? Sally asked.

Smell with your left nostril. It's the river, it has to be! Over there!

They turned a corner onto a larger road and there it was! Leonard had to restrain himself from running to the bridge, which they could see dimly a half a verst ahead.

The Franks were right, because as Leonard and Sally approached the bridge they could see not just the fortress but, across the river and to the left, a magnificent basilica, lit bright—by the torches of a thousand pilgrims.

The river

They were no longer alone: Romans and pilgrims streamed by, converging in groups of two, three, or more from various roads and lanes. Some were ill and barely balanced themselves on wooden crutches, which got caught between the cobbles; others were pulled along in wheelbarrows. A few sang fervently but with little regard to Pythagorean tuning, their eyes fixed on the basilica. A Swedish woman with white hair fell to her knees and cried out to Saint Eric.

I've never seen a river before, have you? Leonard asked.

Sally shook her head.

Do you want to look?

Not particularly, Sally said.

Please?

They stepped away from the road and walked about ten cubits to the riverbank. To the right, they could see the white stone bridge with its five great arches. To the left another twenty cubits, strange floating structures, the purpose of which Leonard could not discern.

It's awfully muddy down here, Sally said.

Leonard nodded, straining now to see what might have been an island connected to the banks by bridges on either side.

I wonder where they find the fish, he said, as he saw no fish catchers.

When Sally didn't reply, Leonard said, It's interesting here, don't you think? Don't you find yourself wondering about this place, its Custom and Commerce, for example? How do the people earn their lucre? What do they eat?

We know what they eat and it's disgusting—and no, I'm not interested to know more. I want to find Felix and get out of here.

Leonard suddenly felt very, very tired.

Don't worry, Sally said. He'll be fine. You trust Isaac, right? He won't let anything happen to him.

No, Leonard said, stepping out of the way of a man and

donkey pulling a creaking wooden cart, its bed filled with sloping sacks of something heavy. They made their way back to the bridge, walking around the four nuns who toddled arm in arm and a blind man who was led by a clubfooted boy. Small groups of pilgrims continued to enter the bridge from every direction, separated by nationality; collectively they surged toward the basilica—funereal Hungarians, Egyptians singing in a low tone. Like a disorganized version of one of the Leader's Birthday Happiness processionals: every group represented, united by hope and joy. All along the bridge, Romans hawked beaded wristlets, tin pilgrims' badges, and disturbing miniature crutches, shackles, and limbs. Instinctively, Leonard and Sally attached themselves to the largest group—ten Portuguese wearing brown pilgrims' gear that more or less resembled theirs—and followed them across the river, where they had their choice of streets to the basilica and chose the busiest.

This must be the Business District, Sally whispered, for indeed, the buildings lining the road were crammed with workshops, stands, and booths, some sheltered by vaulted brick arcades, some jutting into and obstructing the road. They sold many wonders; some even sold lucre—but for what purpose? What manner of strange place this was! In addition to the badges and miniature shackles they'd seen earlier, they now saw books for sale, and straw, and tiny vials of oil—too small for ritual wedding-night anointing (at which thought Leonard blushed)—as well as the more familiar fruit, vegetables, spices, and fish.

Should we talk with the fisherpeople? Sally asked, looking back over her shoulder at a smiling seller of eel.

I think we should wait till morning, Leonard said—and they arrived at a small irregular square, behind which was the basilica, the largest building Leonard had ever seen, larger even than the University Library, though really it seemed a random agglomeration of connected buildings, towers, and outbuildings. Leonard couldn't help but approve of the five flights of seven stairs at the end of the square leading to the main building, five being the quintessence, Pythagoras's marriage number, the indivisible combination of masculine three and feminine two, seven being the virgin prime number, indivisible, with no product within the decad.

As they crossed the square toward the stairs, old men pulled at Leonard's tunic, offering to set broken bones or extract teeth or mend torn-up shoes. Others hawked miniature body parts, blocking their way and pushing wax noses and wooden elbows into their faces. One happy Frisian nearly knocked Sally to the ground after purchasing a model of an ox. Unwashed people, many of them infirm, threw themselves immoderately at their feet, seeming to want coins in exchange for no service whatsoever. Young men swarmed about them, each claiming to be an official guide. Trade jewelry? Trade coins? I get you maximum indulgence! What you speak? German? Frank? Castilian?

Sally and Leonard moved quickly up the steps and elbowed their way through a three-arched structure into a rectangular courtyard surrounded by arcades—it had to be almost a third of a furlong in each direction. Around the sides of the courtyard, ten paintings of large, serene-looking people—the heads of Rome's fast-food joints, perhaps, though Leonard hadn't seen anything like a restaurant yet, apart from Bobolo's hostellery. Through the throng, Leonard could discern—which is to say, he could hear and, eventually, see—two fountains of exquisite beauty. Fantastic birds and sea creatures spouted water into the first from a bronze dome, held aloft by eight red columns (eight, no doubt, because every odd number after one yields a multiple of 8+1 when squared). The second fountain featured a marble bath adorned with lambs, and mysterious symbols ingeniously fashioned out of broken bits of colored stone. Leonard had seen nothing like them, and wished to push away, or at least reprimand, the insolent unwashed who used them to bathe their hands and feet.

Across the courtyard, past the second fountain, was the basilica itself, finally. Hundreds of pilgrims streamed in and out of its five doors, each entryway apparently reserved for some subset of visitor, though there were no pictographs to guide them. Leonard and Sally had nearly walked through a door reserved for Romans, before being pushed away by an angry old man, then one reserved for pilgrims accompanied by their guides. When they finally crammed their way through the correct door, the middle door, which seemed to be made entirely of silver, they felt they had escaped something.

A dark corner where you can think

Once inside, they retreated to a dark corner where they could think. Not that any corner of that brilliantly lit basilica was dark, or quiet enough for thinking. But in the corner at least they ran less risk of being trampled by pilgrims rushing from one extremity of the building to another.

Is this what you expected? Sally asked.

WHAT? Leonard asked.

IS THIS WHAT YOU EXPECTED? Sally asked.

Leonard hadn't expected anything, and certainly not this.

Double aisles flanked each side of an enormous central hall, each aisle marked by columns as tall as any building in the Business District back home. And the length of it—at least one-tenth of a verst! The ceiling was timbered and painted, and along each wall were placed innumerable alcoves, each lit by lamps and decorated with golden objects and paintings of yet more enormous men and women, all, it seemed, wearing what appeared to be gowns. Each of the alcoves was mobbed by pilgrims who clustered and clamored, each trying to touch or kiss the golden objects, or crying out and swooning to the ground. Others held torches and scurried from alcove to alcove. There was no order to their frantic peregrinations as they zigzagged across the aisles, circumventing or, more often, bumping into clumps of pilgrims who picnicked on fish and vegetables or sang songs, accompanied by stringed instruments. This chaos disturbed Leonard perhaps even more than the church's awesome scale and strangeness.

Sally moved closer so they might converse without shouting—so close, in fact, that their tunics touched. Leonard remembered the day before, more than seven hundred years in the future, when Sally's orange-skin gown, in contact with his leg, shimmered like electricity.

He scooched that final inch closer; she didn't seem to mind.

How many people do you think are here? Sally asked, pulling out the last of their provisions: two bridies and two dried ham stix.

A lakh?

Half a lakh, anyway, Sally said, munching on a bridie. The crowd seemed to make her smaller.

I love you, Leonard reminded her, dividing his dried ham stix into five pieces so it might last longer.

I don't like it here, she said in a small voice.

It's not so bad, he said, passing Sally one of the pieces of his dried ham stix. It's like an adventure. Shall we walk around?

I don't want to, Sally said.

We need to know what's here, for security's sake, Leonard said.

Sally couldn't argue with that, though she probably knew that Leonard was merely curious—about those alcoves over there, and what those people were doing over there and there.

I'll come with you, she said. If I don't, you'll lose me and never find me again.

They walked down the aisle that separated the main hall from the outer aisle, thus observing but not participating in the chaos around the alcoves, where the infirm, crippled, and aged discovered new vitality, pushing and shoving and maneuvering with sharp elbows, as did relatives holding stretchers. Others sang boisterously in huddled candlelit circles or read loudly from little books; a few twitched and jerked as if possessed. On the floor and on the walls by the alcoves, Leonard saw the small objects they'd earlier seen for sale—a horse, a chain, a ship—as well as tiny paintings of little pilgrims, their palms pressed together in front of their faces—forgotten, probably, by pilgrims exhausted by their quest.

Crammed between the alcoves were stone figures sleeping on stone boxes—tombs, he heard a guide explain to six red-haired Swabians, and the alcoves were shrines, and the glittering pictures made from colored bits were mosaics. The stone figures were enthusiastically embraced by pilgrims; an old man lay outstretched on one, snoring.

What is that tall lady doing? Sally whispered.

She seems to be sweeping dust from a tomb into a travel pocket.

Can't be.

Leonard had to agree: it couldn't.

Between the shrines and tombs, the walls were covered by richly brocaded throw-cloths, and multicolored orbs tinkled mysteriously against one another; they appeared suspended in air, though in fact they hung from candleholders by tendrils of nearly invisible metal threading.

Why do you like this? Sally asked. I thought you liked your White Room. This is nothing like a White Room.

I did, Leonard said. Maybe because I didn't know places like this existed. Look! he said, and pointed at a brazen figure of a seated man holding a key. Pilgrims were queuing to talk to this figure and to kiss its shiny toe.

Milione was right, he said. The world is full of wonders. You have only to look and pay attention.

Milione?

Another long story.

I'm tired of your long stories.

I'll tell you everything when I can, Leonard said.

I'm tired of everything, Sally said. I didn't nap this afternoon like you did, you know.

We'll rest soon.

Do you think we're safe? Sally asked.

I'm sure of it.

Will you look for signs and wonders, just to be sure?

Leonard put his arm around Sally's shoulder but was tsk-tsked by a nun in a sweeping gray habit.

The strangeness and wonder of the world

And so they circled the great hall, which was actually transected at the far end by a shorter hall, Sally looking over her shoulder all the while for the man with the loud boots or the Frankish woman who thought they were evil, while Leonard marveled at the gilded candle-holding devices that hung ingeniously from the ceiling.

Leonard counted one hundred columns: eighty-eight in four rows separating the central hall from the four outer aisles, plus an additional twelve around the area where the two halls intersected. Again, he approved the decision, one hundred being ten squared, ten being the tetractys, or sum of the only numbers needed to geometrically define known objects (which is to say $1 + 2 + 3 + 4$), but he found perplexing the variety of columns, which were not of uniform size or shape: the two in the front were black, for example, which anyone should know was a mistake.

When they finally returned to their corner, Sally said, Keep looking for signs and wonders, then fell promptly asleep on his shoulder.

Leonard closed his eyes and took a deep breath, and then another, then maybe twenty more, and felt the strangeness and wonder of the world breathing through him in one great circular breath. He remembered Mill's words—you have only to pay attention, to give yourself over to wonder—then opened his eyes and saw, with exquisite precision, clear at the other end of the hall, on a triumphal arch, a mosaic—a mosaic of the building itself, being offered to a scruffy man on a throne, and inside that building, a mosaic of the mosaic within the building, being offered to a man on a throne, and in that mosaic of the building, a mosaic of the building, and so on. All possible mosaics of the building locked into place, and Leonard saw them as if they were one cubit before him, their infinite edges sharp and clear. He looked away and saw the bloody bandage around a pilgrim's head across the basilica; he smelled the man's fear. He closed his eyes and smelled a hundred smells, each of them distinct: incense coiling from every shrine, the smell of the unwashed, every pilgrim with his or her particular scent, the odor of fish dinners, a dozen species of fish cooked according to the customs of a dozen lands. He heard a cacophony of languages; the shriekings and cryings, in all their echoing discord and variety, were as stirring and majestic as the NP theme song. He felt the innumerable gradations of cool marble against his back, and the pressure of Sally's head against his shoulder: sweet Sally!

The world, he murmured, is so beautiful.

Soon it will be no more, a voice said.

Leonard opened his eyes, slowly. A freakishly tall man, bearded and not wholly substantial, hovered before him, his slippered feet not quite touching the ground. He had a pronounced gap between his smiling teeth and was juggling Hebrew letters in the air.

Okay, bye!

How's Felix? Leonard asked. He may have been speaking out loud, it was hard to know.

You understand much, the floating man said. Meditation, extratemporal transportation, fasting . . .

We don't have much food, Leonard admitted. Are you Isaac or Abulafia? he asked.

The man looked hurt.

I am Abulafia, the Messiah. Moshiach? he added when Leonard's face remained blank. The anointed one? Descendant of David? Messenger of peace?

Oh, Leonard said. He wanted to wake Sally—she should see this!—but he no longer felt the weight of her head upon his shoulder—he no longer felt even his shoulder, or his hand, or the marble wall against his back. He wasn't even sure he was breathing.

You're talking kinda normally, he said. Doesn't Isaac translate for you?

Feh! Abulafia said, offended anew. He continued to juggle: an improbable number of letters swirled above his head in complex loops and folderols.

Is Felix okay?

His name is Asher now, and he is fine. I am helping him, he is helping me. You can go home now. Bye! and the man and his swirling letters started to fade away.

I can't leave just yet, Leonard said, and the man returned. I have to see Felix. I have to take him home.

Oh, no. Sorry, the man said, looking up to where he executed a double roundabout juggle that caused the letters to circle each other in both backward and forward motion. That won't be possible. I need him. Big shame! I would have liked to have talked with you about Pythagoras. I met him once, you know, in Tibet. Wonderful man! But now it's time for you to go. Cheerio! and again the man started to fade.

You can't keep him! Leonard said. He's needed at home, we need him at home. He froze the world, you know.

The man returned to focus, looking a trifle put out. His juggle was simple now: just four simultaneous circlings.

It doesn't matter. The world's going to end, Felix will help me. It's a two-man job. So take care now, you hear!

He has to come home.

The spirit-man floated closer, perhaps to impress Leonard with his prodigious height. The letters left his hands and rose to the timbered ceiling, there to loop and spin.

I think you'll find, Mr. Leonard, that Asher prefers to stay with me. So you can go now. Goodbye!

He won't stay with you! Leonard said. He won't. I'll find you. I'll find you and bring him home.

Oh, no! the Abulafia spirit-man said, floating now just inches above Leonard, forcing him to look straight up in the air. The letters were circling his head so fiercely his face could barely be seen. You have to stay away! Why do you think I've come to you? People are already watching us because of you. You were seen, by the Inquisition. You'll bring danger to everyone, Asher included. And get away from this church—there are Orsini everywhere! Okay, it was nice meeting you. Bye!

Before Leonard could ask what an Orsini was, the floating man and his letters had fizzled away.

The sizzling Aleph

But one of them dropped. One of the letters Abulafia had been juggling, it popped out of formation just as the spirit-man dissolved and landed on the marble floor, the coolness of which Leonard could again feel, together with the sweetness of Sally's head upon his shoulder.

The letter smoked a little about the edges, and vibrated. Leonard, not sure what to do, reached for it and put it in his underarm pocket, where the vibration soothed him, so much that despite his intention to protect Sally from Orsini and men with big boots, he went quite thoroughly to sleep.

You look like a Survivalist

I had something of a vision last night, Leonard explained when Sally woke him. A slight vibration under his arm reminded him that Abulafia's letter was still in his pocket. I saw Abulafia. He said they saw us, the Inquisition, that man with the boots, he saw us—I guess when we were running away.

Sally put her hand to her cheek.

That's not possible! What can he have seen? Just the back of us, just the back of two ordinary pilgrims ...

She put her hand on Leonard's afro.

They saw this, she said softly. They think you're wearing crayon-colored sleeping togs, that's okay, but they also saw your hair.

My hair? Leonard said, already feeling the loss.

I can take out my headbeads, but you were running behind me, what they saw is you. We'll have to cut your hair.

The glorious equanimity Leonard had felt the night before, his exaltation over the fecund majesty of the world, was gone; his lower lip trembled.

I can do that, he said.

You're very brave, Sally said. I don't suppose we'll find hair-shears here. You'll have to borrow a knife from those folks over there, the ones who are carving that enormous, delicious-looking loaf of bread. The one with the intoxicating aroma and the oil dripping all over it.

I'm hungry too, Leonard said.

Try not to be conspicuous, Sally said.

Leonard laughed at the idea that any one person in this vast hall of rushing, ecstatic, limping, crying, snoring, shrieking, feasting, singing citizenry might ever be singly conspicuous.

Leonard introduced himself.

The bread-eating family turned out to be Cumbrian.

Ahreet, marra! the elder exclaimed, holding out his hand. Oust fetal? Werst t' frae?

Was this the best Isaac could do? Leonard couldn't understand a word. When he didn't respond, the elder explained to his family, T'boyo's an offcomer, and they nodded knowingly.

Leonard offered multiple gestures. The Cumbrian family gladly lent Leonard their knife, though the youngest and strongest accompanied him to the nearest tomb, where, affecting an ague, Leonard twitched and moaned and cut off his curls, depositing them at the foot of the reclining figure, much to the approbation of a pair of black-robed Sicilian sisters.

The youngest and strongest ran his hand approvingly over Leonard's partially shorn head.

Slape! he said, and Leonard smiled uncertainly.

He gave his thanks to the Cumbrian family. They pointed at their food.

Scran? they asked. Snig? Skemmy? Kets?

Leonard's gaze lingered possibly rather long on their bread, for they gave him one-quarter of it with their blessings.

As he walked off, he heard the youngest and strongest, his hand in his hair, explain to the others: Biddies! he said.

You look like a Survivalist, Sally said, also running her fingers through Leonard's unevenly cropped hair. I like it!

Leonard would willingly have hacked off all his hair on meeting Sally had he known it would please her. And yet, he pondered, such a gesture would have been evidence of neither wealth nor position, nor would it have involved pretty compliments. How puzzling! Milione had been wise about many things, but maybe he didn't know about women.

Or maybe Sally wasn't like most women. Being a paragon, this was, in fact, likely.

I like your new hairstyle, he said.

Sally had removed her headbeads and given them to a Cumbrian child, who was already arranging them in colored polygons on the ground.

They finished their breakfast and stood to go.

Today would have to be the day.

This is your world

They departed the basilica, Leonard taking just one moment to admire the colored window, flower shaped, high above the door, through which entered the most brilliant blue light, and another moment, in the courtyard, to gaze at the gold-backed mosaics— more men wearing gowns—on the church's facade. He was about to point Sally's attention to the tower they'd seen the night before—in daylight he could see that its top was gilded with silver and gold—but Sally sighed. Her expression was downcast, her demeanor despondent.

You feeling any better? Leonard asked.

I'm fine. Why do you ask? Do I seem not fine? I feel fine.

Leonard didn't want to argue with her, so he said, You didn't seem fine last night. Last night you seemed kind of blue.

Sally was about to deny it but didn't. Instead she leaned against one of the fountain's red columns and looked intently at her leather slippers.

This is your world, she said. Not mine. I like things to be clear; I don't like signs and wonders. I don't like being in a world where I don't know the rules, where you have visions I can't see, and some invisible guy named Isaac tells us what to do. Back home, I know how things work: give me a task, and I'll find the best way to do it. Here I do my best and nearly get us killed!

But you've forgotten, Leonard said, standing in front of her and draping his arms over her shoulders.

Forgotten what?

Sally wouldn't look at Leonard: she was still staring at her slippers.

What Isaac said.

What did Isaac say?

That you'll be the one to convince Abulafia to wait . . .

For the birthday of the world . . .

Before visiting the pope!

That's going to be me, isn't it? Sally said, looking up. I had forgotten.

Which doesn't mean you can't figure out what fish have to do with Felix, he said, playing with her unbeaded hair.

What are we waiting for? she said. Let's get to the river!

Soon or someday very soon

Are you getting signs and wonders about which way to go? Sally asked when they reached the river. Around them dank, watery smells hung heavy in the thick summer air.

Abulafia said we should stay away from the church. Something about the Orsini, whatever that is.

The pope is an Orsini, that's his family name. What? she said, smiling. I asked the Brazen Head back in the future. Born Giovanni Gaetano Orsini, pope from 1277 to 1280, died in Soriano, Italy.

He dies?

Sally gave him a look.

It's 1280 right now! Leonard said. Remember? August 1280. Bobolo told us.

He dies this year, then, sometime in the next few months, Sally said.

And we're the only ones who know this, Leonard said.

You don't suppose that . . .

He couldn't, Leonard said. Abulafia? Kill the pope? It's not possible.

We don't know anything about him. Maybe he's a murderer! Maybe your Isaac, whoever he is, sent us to stop a murderer! Leonard, the man has Felix!

Felix has to be okay. Isaac said Abulafia was a good man.

And you trust this Isaac who's been dead forty-five years why?

Because my grandfather trusts him.

Your grandfather who's also dead.

Yes.

And I have to trust them because I trust you?

I guess so.

But you don't trust me enough to tell me about Isaac, or how you talk to people who aren't there.

I'll tell you everything soon.

Soon, really?

Soon. I promise, or if not soon, someday. Someday very soon.

Sally shook her head.

Promise, Leonard said.

The ghastly ghost

They crossed the bridge, again making their way through pilgrims and touts, and began walking along the riverbank in the direction of the island.

What are those things? Sally asked, pointing at the strange floating structures they'd seen the night before.

They walked another twenty cubits toward the nearest, which was made of wood and affixed to a floating dock; on one side, in and above the water, an enormous wheel turned with the current. A loud and unpleasant grinding sound issued from within.

Can't be a fishing station, Sally said, turning her head sideways to get a better view of the wheel. There are no fisherpeople. Or nets, or explosive devices. Do you suppose it's for the amusement of children?

There are too many of them. Must have something to do with Custom and Commerce, Leonard said, and wished Milione were there: assuredly he'd seen perplexities such as these on his travels. It would be nearly twenty years before Mill was back from his travels. Right now, he'd be in the court of Kubilai Khan, or some such place.

I'm going to make sure these aren't fishing stations, Sally said.

What?

I'm going to see!

Careful! Leonard shouted as Sally tripped down the stone path.

Hallooo! she cried, standing at the gangplank that led to the structure. Hallooo! Mr. Fisherperson! I'm looking for some fish! Is Felix here?

A ghostly man stepped out of the first miniature cottage, his face and arms powdered white.

Sally screamed, and ran.

The fisherpersons

Wait, Leonard said, grabbing her as she tore past and pulling her to him. It's okay.

Run! she screamed too close to his ear, struggling to get away.

Sally! It's okay. Look! He's not a ghost. He's a grain smasher.

Ridiculous, Sally said, peeking over Leonard's shoulder at the baffled grain smasher. There are no camels here to rotate the powdering stone.

It's the wheel, he whispered, holding her even tighter. The powdering stone is water powered.

Sally stopped her struggling, but she was shaking and her health meter vibrated. The white-covered man had not uttered a word, was just looking at Leonard and Sally.

I'm afraid of ghosts, she whispered into Leonard's ear. I maybe forgot to tell you.

Leonard had never seen Sally afraid before; she had never needed his comfort. As he stroked her shoulder blades, and smelled the good scent of her hair, and listened to her breath, he thought again of Milione. Everyone fears something, Milione had said. It may not be what you think. The brave person pursues that thing, or at least manages to stand in its midst.

Sally broke away and smoothed her hair.

The grain smasher was still staring.

We're looking for a boy named Felix! Leonard shouted, but the man remained dumb.

We're both tired, Leonard said, leading Sally some cubits away. Shall I check your health meter?

Sally put her hands protectively against her chest.

I'm fine, she said. Absolutely fine. There's nothing wrong with me.

Did you have a bad experience with a ghost once?

It's nothing. Let's go, she said, and started walking ahead. Keep looking for ghosts and wonders, she shouted back at him.

Signs and wonders.

That's what I said, Sally said.

Signs and wonders, yes, Leonard thought. Observe, pay attention, listen. You'll find Abulafia through unmistakable signs.

Wonders were all around, of course. Brick towers; a strange white column taller than any building, against which the sun, barely risen, shone with exotic brightness; the river itself.

Maybe there were too many wonders in this particular world, Leonard thought. Milione never tired of them, but they might flummox a sensitive sort like Sally.

A few cubits ahead, rowboats tied to the bank, some men in rough-cut tunics lingered. Fisherpeople! They had to be.

Sally ran toward them.

Kind sirs!

They saw her and muttered among themselves.

Kind sirs! she said again, drawing closer.

Avast, me hearty! Be ye a strumpet? one of them ventured.

I'm looking for fish, Sally said.

Fish? the man asked. They muttered again among themselves.

You are fisherpeople, right?

Fisherparsons, the leader said, offended.

Also a boy, Leonard added, caught up with Sally. We are looking for a boy.

Arrr! their leader said, thoughtfully. If it be boys yar after, we haven't none of those, not goin' in far that sort of thing. We arrr women-preferrrin' fisherparsons, all of us. But our landlubber matey Petruccio at The Very Olde Sailorparsons' Taverne can help ye, ain't that so?

The other men nodded.

Is it a vary young boy yar after?

His name is Felix, Sally said.

Red afro, Leonard explained. About this high.

Yar tastes are vary partickalar, the leader observed.

Sometimes his name is Asher, Sally said.

Asher! one of the fisherpeople shouted, and again the men conferred in low tones.

Asher! the leader said. You shoulda said so afore! Arrr! He be the lad that assists the Jew magician, over at the fisherparsons' marrrket.

The other men nodded.

I don't think he's far sale, the man added. The others agreed.

And the fisherpersons' market is where?

Whar the fisherparsons sell fish, the leader explained; the others nodded—and, in nodding, seemed to nod in the direction Sally and Leonard were headed. Heartened, they bid their new friends adieu.

Do you think they really were Long John Silvers? Sally asked when they were a safe distance away.

I think Isaac never met a man of the sea.

They giggled. Sally took Leonard's hand. Maybe she was going to be alright.

Talking the pilgrim talk

If the fisherpeople had seen Felix with Abulafia, then he had to be okay. Leonard and Sally would find him and convince him to come home, which shouldn't be hard; Felix would defrost the world, and the three would live happily ever after, with Carol. Leonard almost did a little dance.

I don't think I can come home with you, Sally said.

What? Leonard said.

It's 1280. Roger Bacon is no longer under house arrest—he's studying in Oxford, at the Franciscan House. Don't you see?

You want to visit Roger Bacon?

I want to know what he wrote in the Voynich. I need to know.

Sally, that has to be very far away from here!

I know, I know, I'd have to pass through Cathar territory, it's a problem, but in 1280 they're between Inquisitions. If I can pass as a pilgrim in Rome, I can pass as one returning from Rome, right? I have the gear, I can talk the pilgrim talk. Test me, go on, test me!

Sally, you'd end up in this century forever! I don't know that we could get you home again.

Leonard, I don't have anything to go home to. I've lost my job, my friends, my Special Gift.

You haven't lost your Special Gift! You have a destiny, Isaac said so! You only have to choose it!

Maybe this is my destiny, to find Roger Bacon! He could teach me—I'd belong here, then.

Leonard didn't want to remind her that the pilgrim's journey was a treacherous one, and there was no guarantee she'd find her idol, much less convince him to teach her. Instead, he took her hands and said, It isn't your destiny, my treasure, it isn't. Isaac said nothing about your staying always in the past.

Who is this Isaac? Sally said. Does he care one whit about me? One day I'm reading the Voynich, the fate of the Latter-Day Baconians in my hands, the next day I'm humiliated, my powers gone, forced to run away. A fugitive, all because of this Isaac!

Now I'm in Rome, chasing a man who's probably a murderer, hungry, tired, alone, with no clean undergarments ...

Not alone, Leonard said, wrapping her again in his arms, but he wasn't sure she heard.

So many things

Look, he said, retrieving the shimmering letter from his underarm pocket, wanting to show her a wonder, so she might be heartened. I got this from Abulafia.

The letter seemed to float in Leonard's hand. It was black in color, but contained all colors, just as its hum contained all music.

Sally didn't even look.

Let's get a move on, she said, and walked ahead.

Sally not come home? Leonard's health meter was buzzing. He closed his eyes, practiced a five-second Pythagorean meditation to calm his heart. Then he found himself drawing all his attention together and forming it into a sphere, and then into a perfect ray, and focusing it on the letter—instantly, the world around him blurred and drifted, and in the letter he saw so many things. So many it could have been all the things in the world: his mother on the day she died, fish stewing in Froga's blandreth, pilgrims swarming a shrine, Abulafia juggling letters, a police caravan, a jujuberry bush, Sally forty years from that moment wearing a general's round orange cap and dandling a baby on her knee, her grandson—Leonard's grandson? His granddaughter? He blinked and saw the world as it was just then out of the corner of his eye, and the images were gone.

His own voice

The island just ahead was tightly encircled by grain smashers and fisher camps, and inhabited too by regular folk, which mystified Leonard and Sally, who knew that in a well-ordered society, islands belong to the Leader, lest food chains engage in battle for them. Most of the foot traffic, most of the carts, and, importantly, most of the fish were heading left, away from the island, into lanes surrounded by a mass of buildings. Leonard and Sally followed a fish cart pulled by a man who seemed to know where he was going, past some houses, a few gardens, some shops and towers.

Look! Sally said.

Women were walking in their direction toting small baskets of fish. The smell was unmistakable. And there, in an open square, fisherpeople! Selling all manner of fish on marble slabs balanced on the beheaded tops of ancient columns. Women crowded the fisherpeople, who shouted the unique attractions of their shad, while starveling cats braided themselves around the women's feet, braving pointed boots in hopes of a fish head or tail. But when the fisherpeople cut off a head it went into a basket behind them, which they promptly covered. The cats remained optimistic, however: What choice had they?

Which made Leonard think of Medusa, the neighborly cat: how she would rejoice if she were here! Medusa, who might never really know Sally . . .

Signs? Sally prompted. Wonders?

Leonard half nodded.

I'm not sure you're really trying, Sally said.

What do you expect? he half shouted. You'd rather stay in

this crazy place than come home with me. You don't care one jujuberry about me!

Wait! Sally said. What's that? Listen!

Everyone's always telling me to listen! Leonard shouted. I'm tired of listening! Why doesn't anyone ever listen to—

Leonard was no longer shouting because Sally had covered his mouth.

Listen, she said.

Leonard listened. What he heard was his very own voice.

Leonard hears his own voice

This is what he heard:

I WANT TO SPEAK TO ROGER BACON THROUGH THE BRAZEN HEAD PLEASE.

Followed by a loud voice: BRAZEN HEAD? SOUNDS LIKE IDOLATRY! I SHOULD LIKE TO HARM THIS ROGER BACON, FOR EXAMPLE WITH A **HEAD CRUSHER!**

Sally smacked him hard in the arm.

That's you talking to the Brazen Head! Wait—you spoke with Roger Bacon?

Shh, he said.

What did he say? Did he talk about the Voynich? What did he say?

Sally!

And there was Leonard's voice again, broadcast as if through one of the Leader's mobile shout machines: WHAT IS A CATHAR?

CATHARS? boomed that loud voice. CATHARS BE THE VERY

WORST FORM OF HERETIC! FELLOW CITIZENS, COME! JOIN ME! LET US CAPTURE SOME HERETICS! WE CAN INQUISIT THEM, THEN *ALIENATE THEIR LIMBS!*

Which shout was followed by a murderous ululation—coming from just around the corner!

Run! Sally suggested, so they did.

Stone-bakers

Leonard couldn't say how they ended up there, in a dark road, where their eyes watered from noxious fumes and dust. Inside gloomy shops, one after the other, tired-looking men surrounded by bits of ancient rock tended gigantic ovens, where, it seemed, they were cooking stone.

Stone-bakers. *The world was full of wonders!*

They rested against the arcades.

It was the navigator watch, Leonard said, still puffing. Saying back what I'd said to it. The Inquisitor has the watch.

Obviously.

You're not really mad that I spoke with Roger Bacon. What did you think I did?

Sally shook her head. She seemed close to tears.

Maybe I'm mad that it never occurred to me, okay? I should have thought of that!

Leonard shrugged and realized that if Isaac's plan was to be complete, the Brazen Head would have to shut down, or at least shut down its connection to Bacon, lest someone, maybe even Sally here, call him and reverse Leonard's good work. This saddened him.

You didn't think of it because it was too obvious. Your mind is more subtle than that.

Sally considered this.

Yes, she said, maybe. So what next?

Leonard had no idea. If the navigator watch was talking to the man with the loud boots, it wouldn't just be Leonard's voice and interests it would share—Leonard had been cammed, so they'd also have his face, with or without his ebullient hair.

What else had he asked the Brazen Head? Besides library hours and caravan schedules. He'd asked about Sue & Susheela. He'd asked about Milione, and Isaac. If Dwane were at the other end, he'd suspect that Sally was with him, and know that she'd asked about the pope. He also knew about Sally's Abulafianism.

Wait, he said, how come Dwane isn't frozen?

He's not real, Sally said. He's an early model of the Brazen Head, more successful than Sue & Susheela, but still.

Dwane isn't real and he wants to lead the Baconians?

He thinks he's real.

I thought Dwane created Sue & Susheela.

It's complicated.

Leonard's health meter started to vibrate. Yes, Dwane knew about Leonard and Sally, but he also knew about Felix! Felix was always asking questions of the Brazen Head. If Dwane knew about Felix, then the man with the loud boots knew about Felix, and everything Felix was interested in: avoidance of compost-heap violence, the Talmud, who knows what else! If Dwane still thought Felix was a neo-Maoist traitor spy, it could be Felix the loud-booted man was after, not them!

The navigator watch is our sign, Leonard said. The watch will lead us to Felix.

Sally's cheek

They might catch us, Sally said. Who knows what Dwane's told them.

Leonard took her hand.

It could be dangerous, he said. I'd understand if you didn't come along—and he stroked her cheek.

Uhhh, Sally said in a dreamy voice. I, uh . . .

Felix is my responsibility, Leonard said. You could go find Bacon. I'd understand—and he stroked her other cheek.

Her eyes fluttered shut; she looked like she was thinking about something very far away.

I do care about you, she murmured. I, uh . . . I, uh . . .

Astonished, Leonard stopped stroking her cheek; her eyes snapped open.

Did you say something? she asked. Where are we? What are we waiting for?

A villa in Viterbo

They walked more or less on tiptoe, to the amusement of the stone bakers, who watched them stop every few feet or so to listen. *Nothing.* But the fish market wasn't far—as they crept down the lane they could smell the shad and hear the proudly hawking fisherpeople.

Do you have anything left in your inflatable pocket? Leonard whispered as they arrived at the corner of the market.

I have my house ID scrambler, Sally said. I didn't lose that.

Keep it handy, Leonard said. Hear anything?

They strained their eardrums for sounds of Leonard, or Dwane, but heard only tumult around the corner, and then the man with the very loud voice:

WHERE BE THE MISCREANTS WHO DOTH READ THE HERETICAL TALMUD TOME? I SHOULD LIKE TO HARM THEM, FOR EXAMPLE, WITH A *BRANK!*

Leonard and Sally peeked their heads around the corner. An enormous man with spiked boots and a broad back and a very clean tunic was leaning over a marble stone, shouting at a fisherperson, who was plainly flummoxed.

COME, MADAM, I SHALL NOT HARM THEE, UNLESS IT BE THEE WHO CONCEALETH THE BOY WITH THE EBULLIENT HAIR! SPEAK, MADAM! TELL UGOLINO DE BARBARUBEIS WHERE THE TALMUD READERS RESIDE, AND WHERE I MAY FIND THE BOY!!!

When the fisherperson merely gawped, the enormous man yowled and grasped the marble stone with two colossal fists, upending it, with all its fish, into the mud. He then picked up the terrified fisherperson by the neck and, shaking her, said to the square:

SOMEONE SHALL TELL ME WHERE THESE MISCREANTS BE OR THIS BLAMELESS FISHERPERSON SHALL *DANCE IN A WELL!*

I'll show him wells! Sally said, getting ready to fly at him, but Leonard restrained her.

The dangling fisherperson tried to speak but could only produce a choking, burbling sound.

WHAT? THE FISHERPERSON WISHES TO SPEAK? WHAT SAY THEE? the man asked, and dropped the woman to the ground.

I merely wished to ask, yer honor, that ye release me, I being just then about to expire.

HAST THOU NOT HEARD ME, FISHER WENCH?—but before he

could pick her up again, someone from the crowd shouted: They're in the thee-a-ter, yer honor. I seen 'em sneakin' in, the Jew magician and his redheaded boy.

GOOD MAN! the man with loud boots shouted. THOU SHALT HAVE FROM ME A VILLA IN VITERBO! And off he stomped.

Instruction from a demon

Sally and Leonard followed the man called Ugolino, while also trying to look inconspicuous: Leonard whistled the NP theme song, while Sally feigned interest in fish. When they were well away from the fisherpeople's market, they could hear—was it? could it be?—Dwane, advising Ugolino about ... Abulafia?

Abraham Abulafia was a Spanish mystic of the thirteenth century. He worked with the special characteristics of the Hebrew alphabet—the meanings and sounds and shapes and vibrations of each individual letter. By doing so, he became a great prophet of extraordinary powers.

Familiar words.

I wrote that, Sally said, disgusted.

We need to get the watch back, Leonard said.

Sally nodded.

TRIPE! Ugolino shouted at the navigator watch. I SHALL DO GREAT HARM TO THIS FALSE PROPHET, FOR EXAMPLE, WITH A *FLAIL*!

As you like, they heard Dwane say, *but make sure you get the girl. She's key.*

TRIPE AND MORE TRIPE! Ugolino shouted. THE DAMSEL IS NEVER KEY!

Still, she's bad and I think you ought to hurt her.

I AM ALWAYS DELICATE WITH DAMSELS. WHAT'S MORE, SHOULDST I TAKE INSTRUCTION FROM A DEMON?

Dwane laughed.

Never been cammed

As Ugolino argued with Dwane, he didn't notice Leonard and Sally trailing a block behind him. They soon arrived at a massive rounded edifice consisting of two tiers of dirty brown and white arcades plus a third, walled level up above. The theater, presumably, though Leonard could see no banners or endorsements, no certificates of amusement.

It seemed the people of this town would turn any arcade into a makeshift marketplace: here, swarthy carcass dealers shouted the benefits of their wares and gestured with enormous bloody cutlasses, their aprons smeared with effluvia. At their feet, the inner bits of beasts were gnawed upon by shameless cats.

Leonard had never seen anything so horrifying.

I'm going to stop him, Sally said.

No! Leonard said, grabbing her arm.

He doesn't know my face. I've never been cammed.

The Head didn't cam you?

Why would I let the Head cam me? and she was off behind Ugolino in a flash. Ugolino was pacing before the carcass dealers, shouting something Leonard couldn't hear. Perhaps he was trying to find a doorway large enough to accommodate his gargantuan frame, or determine where he might create one with his fist.

Sally crept up behind him and sprayed the building with her ID scrambler.

Ugolino, alerted by the spraying sound, stepped back, bumping into Sally, who sprawled to the ground.

DEAR LADY PILGRIM! he exclaimed. I AM MOST HEARTILY CHAGRINED. ALLOW ME TO HELP THEE TO THY PRETTY FEET!

Are you looking for something? she asked, once upright, slipping the ID scrambler into her clutchbag. Can I direct you to another place very far away?

WHY, YES, PRETTY LADY PILGRIM! I HAD THOUGHT THIS TO BE THE THEATER OF MARCELLUS, FORTRESS OF THE SAVELLI, WITH ITS CURVATURED FRONT AND REINFORCED ARCADERY. HOW SADLY I AM MISTAKEN. MANIFESTLY IT IS A MUNICIPAL COMPOST HEAP VERY NEAR THE BASILICA OF ST. PETER'S!

The thronging pilgrims should be a clue, Sally said.

Ugolino looked around, confused.

YES! he shouted. I'M SURE I SHALL NOTE THEM MOMENTARILY. HAST THOU SEEN THE BOY WITH THE EBULLIENT HAIR?

He is definitely at the theater, Sally said. I saw him there myself. Causing mischief and spouting heresy. A verst down the river that-a-way, across the bridge, left at the castle fortress. You can't miss it.

VERY GOOD, LADY PILGRIM. CANST THOU OFFER ME A KISS TO CHEER ME ON MY WAY?

I think you're in a hurry.

Ugolino nodded and was about to stomp off when his wrist cried out.

That's her! I hear her voice! It's Sally! Kill her! Hurt her! Kill her!

Ugolino turned to Sally, his confusion rapidly turning to rage. He ululated and lifted his arm as if to strike her, then crumpled mightily to the ground.

Hoarfrost

Leonard had smacked Ugolino's head with a paving stone, causing much murmuring among the carcass dealers. He now grabbed Sally and commenced to shouting:

Abulafia! Abulafia! You have to let us in! Quick! Quick! We have to talk!

Zedekiah appeared from the shadows behind the arcade and pulled them both after him, through a door into a dank, dark hallway.

Abulafia is going to have to take care of him now, Zedekiah said. You realize that? And maybe all of those carcass dealers!

What do you mean? Sally asked.

You led him here, putting us all in danger.

He led us, actually.

He is here because of you, and now Abulafia must attend to him.

Meaning what? Leonard asked.

Better not to know, Zedekiah said, then flattened himself against the wall as a freakishly tall man—or maybe a rushing spirit?—flew past them, opened the door, and touched the prostrate Ugolino with a disgusted fingertip. After muttering a few unintelligible words, the man-spirit disappeared. Into the thinnest air, taking Ugolino with him. In a moment he was back, slamming the door behind them, and again streaming past.

He was covered in hoarfrost, Ugolino nowhere in sight.

My Master says there are regions so cold that moving things lose their life there. They become still as statues. Even water ceases to move. I know! Most remarkable! He has brought that terrible man to such a place.

Abulafia left Ugolino on a polar tip?
Come this way, Zedekiah said.

The End of Days

What is this place? Leonard asked, as they walked down the narrow stone hallway, with its uneven floor, grooved by centuries of walking.

In the old days it was a theater, Zedekiah said, over his shoulder.

So I gather.

Now it is a fortress. It belongs to the Savelli, Zedekiah said.

Name sounds familiar, Sally said.

No relation to Bobolo, more's the pity. Watch your head.

They ducked under a low-hanging lintel and walked up first one, then another flight of stairs.

The Savelli are no friends of the Jews, Zedekiah said, but they hate the Orsini more. They know of the Master's plan to visit the Orsini pope ...

Nicholas III, Sally said, stopping at the top of the stairs.

They are hoping the Master will kill him, Zedekiah said, also stopping. Or shock the pope to death with his wondrous signs, or maybe send him to a far-off world. They hope one of their own can then be elected in his place. They've had rather a dry spell, pope-wise. They delude themselves, of course. When the Master visits the pope, it will be to announce and, by announcing, effect the End of Days.

The End of Days? Leonard asked.

The End of Days! Zedekiah confirmed.

Awesome karate kicks

Leonard gave Sally a tender shove so she'd start walking again.

Where's Felix? Leonard asked.

Young Asher is fine, Zedekiah said. How could it be otherwise? He is learning with the Master.

Why didn't you just tell us where he was? Why confound us with riddles? Sally asked.

You said you were guided, Zedekiah said. It was important to know if this was true.

Why *Asher*? she asked.

The boy needed a Hebrew name. Obviously. *Asher* means happy, like *Felix*. For someone who is guided, my lady, you seem to know very little.

You're not speaking as you were before, Sally observed.

Zedekiah looked at them blankly. The man was now within Abulafia's realm, Leonard realized; the translation, somehow, came from him, not Isaac. This made Leonard uneasy: could Isaac not reach them here?

He wished he had a plan, but he was out of plans.

Zedekiah led them into an anteroom and motioned them to sit on some wooden benches.

Not till I see Felix, Leonard said.

He and the Master are studying. You have seen what the Master is capable of. Interrupt him, and he could lose concentration, and who knows where they might end up, he and the boy. Best to wait. Please, sit. *No, not together!*

Leonard and Sally sat on separate benches.

Reading material is here, if you are feeling worshipful, Zedekiah said, pointing to some leather-bound tomes with golden Hebrew writing on their covers. They looked very much like the books Leonard's grandfather read, only newer. One, on top, was very small and featured silver cornerpieces. Leonard was about to reach for it, to see the patterns stamped on its leather exterior, when Zedekiah said, It is possible to watch the learning.

Leonard jumped up, and Zedekiah showed him a small peeping hole in the varnished wood door.

This is what Leonard saw:

Felix looking on while a freakishly tall bearded man with a space between his teeth practiced awesome karate kicks.

He's laughing

Sally! Leonard shouted. He's there! Felix is there! He's laughing.

Laughing at the Master? Zedekiah said, pushing Leonard away. This is not possible. Enough. Sit back down. You are not initiated.

Not initiated! Leonard said. I taught the boy everything he knows! and to Zedekiah's infinite surprise, and possibly his own, he too began to kick.

When he finished, Zedekiah's face was white, and Leonard's was bright red.

I insist on seeing the boy *this very minute*!

I'll see what can be done, Zedekiah muttered, and left the room through a door that seemed to lead in an entirely different direction.

Come look, Leonard said to Sally.

I trust you, Sally said.

Leonard looked again through the peeping hole. Abulafia was still kicking, his face ecstatic; Felix was watching a miniature sundial near a window, apparently shouting encouragement. On a low table, near the Master, what looked to be a navigator watch; under the table, carrying bags.

Zedekiah was nowhere in sight. This is ridiculous, Leonard thought, so he simply opened the door.

There was no rending of the universe, no disappearing into alternative space realms. Instead, Felix shouted, **Leonard!** and Abulafia, losing his concentration, lost his balance and landed on an elbow.

Leonard wasn't sure what to do first: hug Felix or check whether Felix had stopped yet another world.

He hugged Felix, of course, who said, Don't worry, I didn't stop the world. Abba taught me how to control my powers. It's not hard once you know how. Or at least some of my powers— we don't even know how many I have! What happened to your hair? Is Sally here? Hi, Sally!

Abulafia picked himself up from the ground.

I believe you have something of mine, he said.

Leonard ignored him.

We've come to take you home, he said to Felix.

Something small, Abulafia said. I need it back, *we* need it back. Tonight, in fact.

I can't go home yet, Felix said. We're bringing on the End of Days, then I can go home.

Felix, angel button, if you bring on the End of Days, there will be no home.

Felix looked up at Abulafia quizzically. The Master must have been three times Felix's height. He knelt down so he could look Felix in the eye.

Technically, your uncle is correct, he said. But the End of Days is far better than anything, you'll see.

Okay, Felix said. Leonard, you won't believe the things I can do! Abba says that when I stop time, I'm at the edge of the orchard! He knows the secret of the orchard! He knows what the Bens, the rabbi, and the other guy saw there! He's the rabbi who saw what was there and went home again!

Abulafia rose again to his full height.

The orchard is the mystical secret of everything, it is that toward which we ascend, we prophets. The unworthy cannot bear it—they die, they go insane or become heretics. You can see this thing, boychik, if you stay with me.

Don't you call him that! Leonard warned.

He says I'll see it too! Felix said.

But we have to leave now if we're to see the pope tomorrow and be back before the Sabbath, Abulafia said, picking up his carrying bag. My small thing? he asked. Maybe you can give it to me now before you forget?—and he started inching toward Felix.

Leonard grabbed the boy.

Oh, no, Leonard said. Felix is finished with you. He's coming home with us.

Aww, Leonard! *Aww!* C'mon!

Felix stomped his little foot.

I don't *wanna* go home! You can't *make me*!

It's not going to work, Sally said. Abulafia, it's not going to work.

All turned toward Sally. Abulafia put down his bag.

What do you mean? the mystic said. Of course it's going to work—and he raised his arms over his head. I am the Messiah, *moshiach,* the anointed one, descendant of David, messenger of peace! I will share holy signs and wonders with the pope *and he shall see!* The End of Days shall be upon us! Glory, glory! Only I need my aleph, if you don't mind—and he extended a hand to Leonard.

No, Sally said. Don't you see? If you bring on the End of Days, how can you explain our being here?

You are sent here to annoy me. By Isaac the Blind, who doesn't want me sharing secrets with the pope, this I already know. He is jealous. ***GIVE ME MY ALEPH! PLEASE!*** Do not make me send you to the land of frozen things!

No, Sally said, you're not thinking. Where do we come from?

You come from an undiscovered land, this I already know.

Yes, but when? What time do we come from?

Abulafia leaned against a low table and scrutinized Sally.

Can you rephrase the question?

We come from the future, Leonard said.

Stuff and nonsense, Abulafia said, though he didn't look so sure.

It's true, Sally said. Far, far in the future. More than seven hundred years.

Fiddle-dee-dee, Abulafia said, looking from Sally to Leonard and back again, waiting for one of them to concede the joke. You are serious?

Utterly, they said in unison.

You must prove this thing to me.

Leonard and Sally looked at each other.

The navigator watch, that can only be from the future, right? Leonard said, inching toward the watch on the table.

I am willing to believe, he said, shifting a step or two to his left so he could stand between Leonard and the watch, that undiscovered nations produce wonders in our very day that are unknown to me.

Ask Felix, Sally said. You know he doesn't lie.

Yes, Leonard said, ask Felix. Felix, you must tell Abulafia the absolute truth.

Yes, Felix said. We come from the future. Can I show my uncle a trick?

All the air seemed to escape Abulafia's arms and legs. He lowered himself to the floor and slumped over his long limbs, hopelessly tangled.

If you come from the future, he said softly, his head in his hands, then I cannot usher in the End of Days and I am not the Messiah. The world cannot end *and* produce a future.

He looked so dejected, he seemed to have shrunk four sizes.

And the pope will kill me, he added.

I can help, Sally said.

You cannot help, Abulafia said, so deflated his forehead almost touched his toes. I will go—I must, or too many will lose their faith. But he will definitely kill me.

I can help, Sally said. If you follow my instructions, I can guarantee your safety.

Abulafia shook his head.

There can be no helping me. Who am I if I am not the Messiah, *moshiach*, anointed one, descendant of David, messenger of peace? What is my purpose if not to bring on the End of Days? Be quiet, I must meditate on this.

He straightened his back and closed his eyes. Leonard had never seen anyone sit quite so *stilly* before.

Sally and Leonard looked at each other.

He can sit like that a long time, Felix said.

Really?

Felix nodded.

Sally approached him.

Mr. Abulafia? she shouted into his ear. Mr. Abulafia? I can help you!

That won't help, Felix said.

Mr. Abulafia! Time is running out! You need to listen!

Sally prodded the master's shoulder. He swayed but did not attend.

You've seen this before? Leonard asked Felix.

Felix nodded.

How long does it last? What brings him out of it?

Felix shrugged and looked at his toes.

You know, don't you?

It's embarrassing.

Embarrassing? Leonard asked. How can you be embarrassed with us? We love you more than anyone anywhere, except your mother, right?

Just yesterday, your uncle here ran through ancient Rome in crayon-colored sleeping togs. All the girls tittered, but he wasn't embarrassed, were you, Leonard?

I'm not sure they tittered, exactly.

They tittered! Sally said, and Felix giggled.

Just this afternoon, Leonard said, Sally here, who has to be the bravest girl ever, got scared of a man covered in wheat flour. She thought he was a ghost!

Felix smiled. Sally glared.

You weren't embarrassed, were you, Sally? Not in front of me, right?

Sally considered this.

No, she said, I wasn't.

Why are you afraid of ghosts? Felix asked.

It's complicated, Sally said.

Felix waited.

The kids at school, Sally said, they used to make me sit on the municipal compost heap till after dark, then they scared me with white sheets. I was very little.

Didn't you have an uncle to take care of you?

No, Sally said. I didn't have anyone. Not anyone. I would have nightmares but no one noticed.

No one? Felix asked.

My parents, well, they were busy, she said, and maybe her voice faltered.

Leonard squeezed Sally's hand; she squeezed it back.

So what is it? Leonard asked Felix. No embarrassment. What makes Abulafia wake up?

He wakes up when I tell him stories, Felix said. He likes to hear about Princess Celeste.

The Princess Celeste

Felix said storytelling always worked better on Leonard's knee, so Leonard sat on a wooden bench and Felix climbed onto his lap.

Abba says Celeste is really the Shekhina, and the compost heap is the unredeemed material world, Felix explained.

Ah! Leonard said, squeezing Felix.

You start, Felix said.

Me? Leonard asked.

Yes, Felix said. The stories are better when you tell them.

Oh, Leonard said. Okay.

He looked at Sally, who waited attentively.

Who should our story be about today? Leonard asked. And Felix said, A beautiful princess named Celeste! and Leonard said, Oh, and where does Celeste live? and Felix said, In a great wooded land surrounded by beasties! and Leonard said, Beasties, oh my! and Felix, his pale cheeks pinkening, said, They're terrible! They like to dump little boys onto the municipal compost heap! And on it went.

Abulafia opened his eyes.

What happens next? he said.

Sally's plan

I have a plan for you, Mr. Abulafia, Sally said.

I'm listening, Abulafia said glumly. Neither his meditation nor Felix's story had improved his spirits.

First you must give us the watch, Sally said.

Abulafia looked at her blankly.

The demon in the reliquary, Leonard explained.

Abulafia nodded listlessly. Leonard took the watch from the low table and strapped it to his wrist. It was still cold, and on its face Dwane's head was frozen and covered with hoarfrost, though the icicles on his chin had started to drip. Leonard pressed the Go to Sleep button to silence Dwane, but the button seemed to have frozen—once defrosted, Dwane might say anything! Leonard nodded to Sally in a way that suggested urgency.

How many days before the birthday of the world? she asked Abulafia.

Five, Abulafia said.

Good number! Leonard said, approving.

But you're leaving today, correct?

Correct. The plan was to convert the pope and be back in time for the Sabbath.

Does your plan still matter now that you know the world will not end?

Of course it matters! A Jewish pope? We would all be safe then.

Okay, Sally said. Well, the birthday of the world must be a powerful time.

Naturally, Abulafia said. Rosh Hashanah is the Day of Remembrance, the Day of Judgment, the day on which we are inscribed in the Book of Life, when our holy shofar cracks open the heart, and the Gates of Heaven.

Visit the pope on that day, then, Sally said. The Franciscans may imprison you for a few days, but you will be okay. I promise.

How do you know this?

The Birthday of the World will protect you, Sally said. I know this from the future.

Abulafia nodded.

I met many Franciscan followers of Joachim in Sicily, he said. I shall be safe with them. Then he looked up, seeming to wake from his miserable haze.

The boy must come with me. I need him.

No, Sally said.

You would keep him against his will? Leonard asked.

Of course not, Abulafia said, standing, but he wishes to stay. Can I, Leonard? Oh, can I?

Felix, we have to go home. If we don't go now, you'll be here forever.

Oh, no!

Asher, you like it here, don't you? You like the games we play and the things I show you?

Oh, yes!

You will never see me again, Felix, or your home, if you decide to stay, Leonard said.

You will never find another teacher like me, Asher. Know this for sure.

Felix, you froze the whole world, you even froze yourself!

I did?

You will learn to do even more marvelous things if you stay with me, Asher. No one will ever toss you onto a dung heap again.

Compost heap, Sally said.

Are you going back too, Sally? Felix asked.

Sally didn't reply.

You need a teacher, Asher. Know this: For fifteen years I was tormented because I had no one to guide me. The dung heap was nothing compared to the torture I endured. I was like a blind man. I will not let this happen to you.

Leonard? I want to stay! Can't you stay too?

Felix, your mommy needs you.

Mommy? My mommy needs me?

She was injured the night you froze the world, Leonard said. Do you remember? She needs a healer, except all the healers are frozen.

Felix began to cry.

You are lying! You must prove this thing, Abulafia challenged.

If I can prove this thing, and the boy wishes to leave, will you agree to help us return? Leonard said. I will then give back to you what you lost.

Abulafia scoffed. I will do this thing, he said, though you will not do that thing.

Leonard is an honest man! Sally said. Even when he isn't, he is!

Leonard smiled at her gratefully and sat on the ground, pretzeling his legs in Pythagorean fashion. He looked at the watch: the hoarfrost had melted from Dwane's head, revealing inflamed facespots. Dwane's eyes were blinking and shifting this way and that, as if he were trying to orient himself.

Come, Felix, sit on my lap. Quickly, please. Sally, hold on to my shoulder.

Once Felix and Sally were in place, Leonard cautioned them to be absolutely still and quiet. He pulled the aleph out of his underarm pocket. It shimmered black and all colors, it hummed all music, it smelled like revolutionary stew and all possible odors, both pleasing and vile, in all possible combinations. Leonard closed his eyes, did a five-second Pythagorean meditation, then gathered his thoughts, as well as the thoughts he was about to have, and might have had, and probably would never have, and concentrated them into an absolute point, hard and sharp as a diamond, and with that diamond inscribed the word *Carol* into his mind's eye, then looked deep into the depths of the aleph—and there she was!

Felix gasped. Carol as a baby, a girl, Carol playing her clarinet, getting the news about their parents, Carol watching Joseph walk away with his oboe, Carol kissing their grandfather, and Leonard, and Felix as they slept, Carol cooking her Chicken-in-Every-Pot Pie and making Felix go outside to play, Carol sneaking out of the house in her climbing suit, Carol storming the Baconian safehouse, tripping in the Business District, being beaten by a justice stick, Carol curling into the classic defensive position, being carried through a frozen world, unconscious in her wheelbarrow, lying, unmoving now, in Leonard's bed. Unmoving, still unmoving, always unmoving . . .

Does the aleph ever lie? Leonard asked Abulafia.

Never, the man said.

I need to go home, Felix said, sobbing. I need to fix my mother.

Sorry, Mr. Abulafia.

Just Abulafia, please.

Sorry, Abulafia, Leonard said, and looked at the watch. Dwane was confused, his mouth opening and closing like a fish.

Time for us to go, he said. Goodbye, Mr. Abulafia. Come on, guys.

I need to say goodbye to Zedekiah, Felix said.

No you don't, Leonard started to reply, but he was interrupted by Dwane's reedy voice:

Kill the girl! She's a liar! She's evil! Kill the girl! She's a heretic! She's evil! The boy is a false prophet. Kill the boy! Kill them both!

What is this? Abulafia said, looking left and right. He didn't seem to understand that the voice came from the watch. Am I having a vision? What mystery is this? What am I to understand?

Ugolino! Kill the girl! Ugolino! Kill the girl! Dwane cried.

Why do you call me this, Master? Abulafia cried, addressing the ceiling. It is I, Abulafia, Your faithful servant! Is this a sign? If only I had my aleph! Master, I thought I was to be Your Messiah! Tell me, Master, how have I displeased You?

Abulafia! Dwane said in a scheming voice. Why, yes, you've displeased me! Kill the girl, and you will please me.

Abulafia looked stricken, paler than his usual pale.

Is she to be my Isaac? Shall a ram appear to save me from heinous murder?

Abulafia had plainly gone mad—madder than mad, even! Leonard had to do something, but what?

I do not believe you wish this of me, Master! Abulafia said, still addressing the ceiling.

I do wish this! Dwane shouted. I wish this very very much! Kill the girl! Kill the girl! And the child! And the Stan with the big hair.

No one here matches that description, Abulafia said.

Sally grabbed the watch from Leonard's hand and shouted, Go away, Dwane! We don't need you here, Abulafia doesn't need you.

My name is not Dwane! Dwane shouted. Kill the girl, kill the girl! I am your master, Abulafia, I command you!

Abulafia looked at Sally rather apologetically.

The voice is unequivocal, he said.

Dwane's face was puffed and purple from the exertion of shouting and hating.

Look! Leonard said, putting the watch in Abulafia's face. This isn't your master, this is a face-spotted boy named Dwane.

Abulafia looked at Dwane and gasped.

That is not my master! he murmured.

That's what I said! Leonard said, clapping Abulafia on the back.

This is one of the demons! Abulafia said. I *am* the Messiah! You have been false with me! This is one of the demons I must defeat in order to bring on the End of Days. I am ready for this ultimate battle! I had thought it would be in the presence of the pope that I would do this marvelous thing, but I am ready now!

I don't understand, Sally said.

I am a demon! Dwane shouted. Kill the girl! Kill the girl!

We Masters of the Name, Abulafia said, use demonic ethers to attain prophetic states and transport ourselves, as well you know. The misuse of these powers by the uninitiated threatens the tender balance between good and evil in our world—your blind rabbi has dedicated himself to preserving that balance, precisely so that the Messiah—so that *I*—can defeat the forces of evil when the time is right. And the time is right, it is now! If the world were not about to end, I'd point you to Rabbi Isaac ben Yakov Ha-Kohen, who has written of this most eloquently in his *Treatise on the Left Emanation.* Please excuse me, gentlemen and lady, I must prepare myself for the final struggle ... and Abulafia started toward the door.

Don't forget to kill the girl! Dwane shouted.

Wait! Leonard shouted after Abulafia. First let this *thing* prove itself to be who he says he is. What is your name, demon? Leonard challenged. And you can't ask the Brazen Head.

I, uh, I, uh.

You don't know your name! Leonard called out. Come on, *Dwane*, what's your name?

I, uh.

Even this small child here knows the names of all the demons in the third ether, don't you, Felix?

I do, Felix said.

One last chance, Leonard said, as Abulafia approached to look again at Dwane's face, which was the very picture of befuddlement. Who is the king of the third ether?

That's easy! I am! Dwane said, smiling. I am the king-of-everything demon!

Trick question! Leonard said. Felix, do the clapping song with me, and Felix did.

Who is the king of the [*clap*] third ether?
Trick question!
There are [*clap*] three parts to the [*clap*] third ether!
Asmodeus is the king of the [*clap*] upper ether! *And Lesser Lilith is his wife!*
Kafkaphony is the king of the [*clap*] middle ether! *And Kafkaphony has two wives!*
Sarita is his wife for the [*clap*] first six months! *Sagrirta is his wife for the second!*
Kafsephony is the king of the [*clap*] bottom ether! *And Mehetzabel is his wife!*
Who is the king of [*clap*] *all* the demons?
Samael is the king of [*clap*] all the demons! *And great Lilith is his wife!*
Oh, yes, Samael is king of [*clap*] all the demons. *Samael is king of them all!*

The demon is a fraud, Abulafia said. I am sorry I doubted you. I am also glad I don't have to kill you.

Sally, who had never heard the song, was astonished.

I *knew* you knew about the third ether—why wouldn't you tell me! Felix's drawing, the one he made for me, it was a drawing of the demons—I knew it was! It matched what I read from the Voynich! Bacon probably studied with your Mr. Kohen!

Bacon? Abulafia said. Feh! I don't eat this trayf.

I was all alone, Sally said to Leonard. I was the only one who could see what I saw. I told you and you made me think I was crazy!

It was Isaac, Leonard said. He didn't want you to know. He said you had to choose your destiny first, before you could know.

I can't believe you didn't tell me! I hate you, Leonard! I hate everything about you!

It wasn't me! Leonard said, horrified, his ears turning red.

I hate you wholly and completely! I lied before: you looked stupid running through the streets in your sleepsuit, you should have been embarrassed! I hate you!

I still think you should kill her, Dwane said.

Shut up, Dwane! Sally said, grabbing the watch from Leonard's hand. You're finished! I'm finished with all of you—*all of you!* I'm going to find Roger Bacon and never see any of you ever again!

Me too? Felix asked.

You can't get rid of me! Dwane said.

I can! Sally said. I should have done this ages ago.

Hit me with your best shot! Dwane said, and giggled.

I have a question for the Brazen Head! she said. Bring me the Brazen Head!

A small whirring came from the watch. Leonard looked over Sally's shoulder: the Head was sitting on his velvet throne and picking his teeth with a gold toothpick.

Brazen Head! I want you to find evidence that Dwane is real. Go! Now!

The Head dropped his toothpick. He stared at Sally.

"Please repeat the question. The Head is having difficulty comprehending."

You heard me! Sally shouted. Bring me any evidence you can find that Dwane is real. Go! Now! You're not allowed to do any other work until you find me this evidence.

The Head's face became red; steam began to issue from its ears.

It will take him three eons and a millennium, she said. He will never find proof and he will never stop looking. After three eons and a millennium, his mechanism will die.

You! Abulafia said. The three turned to him. He was looking quite fiercely at Sally.

I can't believe I didn't see it before, he said. You also have the gift. I did not know this was possible in a woman. Three in one room? By all rights the world should have broken apart.

He may have been making a joke, but no one was laughing.

It hasn't broken apart because you haven't yet learned to use your powers, Abulafia said. Not fully. I can help you. You also see the letters dancing, don't you? You are the sole descendant of Ezra ben Solomon, the elder of Isaac's two disciples. I can see this now. This is why Isaac is so interested in you. But he wants to control you, dear lady; I want to teach you! Shall I teach you? I can teach you to read those dancing letters—better yet, I can teach you to *make* them dance! Alone, you will achieve nothing, alone your Special Gift means nothing! Together, there will be nothing you and I cannot do!

Sally's face turned white. She looked first at Abulafia, then at Leonard.

I, uh . . . , she said.

You will be a great leader, Abulafia continued. I see who you are now: a leader! You surround yourself with books, but you are meant to lead armies! That is your destiny. To lead the army of the faithful in the ultimate fight against evil! You do not need this one here, he said, referring to Leonard. Leonard fulfilled his destiny simply by being here, in my presence, and caring for that boy. You are destined to do so much more, and you will, with my help. Together, you and I can be the Messiah.

We can? she said.

Sally, Leonard said, I need to show you something, and he stroked Sally's cheek.

Again her eyes fluttered; she looked like she was thinking about something very far away.

I know you're mad at me, Leonard said, but please look at one thing before you make up your mind—and he stroked her other cheek. It wasn't fair, but he had no choice.

Sally?

Mute, Sally nodded, and Leonard removed his hand from her cheek.

What? she asked. What's going on?!

Look, Leonard said, and he concentrated his thoughts into a diamond, and with that diamond etched the song of his heart onto the aleph, so that in it, Sally could see *herself.* Leading an army—not of strange people from the Middle Ages, but of people she understood, *her* people: barbecuties and Survivalists and flamethrowers, Dada Diner hashslingers and Luddite bakers, friars, alchemists, and optics researchers, wagonette drivers, librarians, and policemen with justice sticks—Cathars, even. She was their leader!

You will always have your Special Gift, Leonard murmured into her ear. You *are* your Special Gift, you are *our* Special Gift. Roger Bacon can't give you anything you don't already have, neither can Abulafia. This here, this is your destiny.

Sally kept looking. She saw the power of Ezra combine with the power of Azriel in a cascade of exquisite explosions. She saw knowledge enter the world, and justice.

There's more, Leonard said. Look. You will never be lonely. You will never be alone, not ever again.

She saw herself as a white-haired woman wearing a general's round orange cap, bobbling on her knee . . . a child, *her granddaughter*, she saw so much joy. A child with ebullient hair and headbeads, who juggled letters and numbers, making the most glorious patterns. The child, this grandchild, looked at Sally through the aleph's clear haze and smiled.

Okay, Sally said. I'm ready. I'm ready to go home.

AFTERWORD

Meow, said Medusa

The mechanics of how they returned are not important. Suffice it to say, there was a circle, a mixing of letters in Sally's head, a silent singing by Leonard of the clapping song, some hopping and dancing according to a well-established pattern, and a mysterious extra ingredient provided by Abulafia, which Sally and Leonard could neither see nor hear.

As they hurtled, motionless, through space-time, Felix saw a time when he was no longer dumped onto the municipal compost heap, when he and his mother read from his great-grandfather's books together, and he filled his opus with accounts of what he'd seen in a script no one but he and Sally could understand. Sally saw Isaac's purpose, and all of Leonard's journeys. She saw herself organizing a freedom army to establish a postdenominational society where no citizen would be judged by the food they ate. Leonard saw Isaac, who still spoke to him in the voice of his grandfather: Boychik, he said, you did good, you did very very good, you saved the world *again*, you are a good egg, and that Sally of yours, she's a good egg, and Felix, now you know: he will never share that opus with anyone but the grandchildren. This was the most important thing we ever ever do. You listening? I'm glad you're listening, because there's this Moses de Leon in Spain, your trip to Rome sent psychic waves all bananas over to him and now he's talkin' to Shimon bar Yochai eleven centuries before, and we gotta do somethin'. You in? Isaac asked, and Leonard nodded his insubstantial head outside of time and space, which Isaac seemed to understand.

And in less time than it took for a cat to blink, they were home.

Meow, said Medusa.

An Interview with the Author

Jewish mysticism plays a large part in *A Highly Unlikely Scenario*, from the characters of Isaac and Abulafia to the clapping song to the idea of *ibburs* and gilguls. Where does your interest in mysticism come from, and how have you pursued it?

Every year for about ten years I went on a meditation retreat led by some very interesting rabbis who often talked about Jewish mystical ideas, which I then read more about on my own. In particular, they introduced us to some of Abulafia's mystical practices, which involve combining Hebrew letters with vowels in particular patterns. These are concentration practices, but also practices of the body, as you breathe in and out with the letters. We learned that these were powerful practices, not to be engaged in lightly or shared willy-nilly with others. It was, in fact, one of these rabbis who inspired *A Highly Unlikely Scenario* by mentioning (offhandedly?) the incredible proliferation of mystical thinking in the thirteenth century, which is when Abulafia and Isaac the Blind lived. But Jewish mysticism is filled with wonderful ideas—I don't think I'm done exploring them in fiction.

Another of your interests appears to be the history of science, including figures like Roger Bacon. Is there something about the omnivorous intellectual curiosity of people like Bacon, who studied optics, astronomy, mathematics, and possibly flying machines (not to mention philosophy and theology), that appeals to you?

There's something compelling about thinkers—I won't call them Renaissance figures, because Roger Bacon was definitely a medieval man—who are interested in *everything*, who see the connections in *everything*. Bacon is one of those early scientific figures who doesn't see neat separations between the material, the spiritual, and the intellectual, and who finds explanations offered by alchemy or theology to be just as compelling as those offered by optics or engineering. He actually did construct a head made of brass (a brazen head) that was meant to serve as oracle. Who wouldn't want to write about such a figure?

The world of the novel is meticulously detailed, from the food, clothes, and hairstyles to things like the Hello! lamps on Everything's-Okay poles. Did you have this particular setting in mind, or did you invent aspects of it as you went along?

Everything about the book's invented setting evolved with the book; coming up with these details was one of this book's great pleasures. Nothing is more fun than starting a sentence not knowing how it will end. While some aspects of the book had to be more controlled, even in the first draft—the cosmology, the three-part structure—most of the details could be invented spontaneously. The Scottish dishes prepared by Carol's restaurant, however, are all real, and none are probably bite-size!

You spent some of your childhood in Rome. Did you draw on those memories when you were portraying medieval Rome in the book? What's your favorite place to visit in Rome?

A lot of the Roman setting did come from memory—most notably, the itinerary Sally and Leonard follow as they travel around the city: to the river, across the bridge, past the Castel Sant'Angelo, to the old St. Peter's, down the river, past the island to the Portico of Octavia (the fish market), and on to the Theater of Marcellus. There's not a lot left in Rome that's medieval, though, apart from some churches, so I also looked over old maps and read books about the medieval city—its pilgrims, architecture, daily life, weapons, the Inquisition, the Jewish population, and so on. The St. Peter's in the book, for example, is the old St. Peter's, which was demolished to make room for the basilica, of Michelangelo fame, that we now see. My favorite Roman places did not make it into the book: the multileveled San Clemente church, for example; or Trastevere, the neighborhood where I grew up; or the flea market at Porta Portese. As well as numerous *pizzerie* and *gelaterie*!

One of the most poignant relationships in the book is the one between Leonard and his grandfather, especially as Leonard realizes what his grandfather was trying to get across to him all those years, with his stories and strange questions. And in a more general sense, the novel seems especially concerned with different generations learning to understand and appreciate each other. I guess what I'm asking is: do you have nephews with magical powers and a grandfather who likes herring?

Hah! I do have nieces and nephews—four, at last count—each as precocious and precious as Felix, if not more so. This book is dedicated to them, in fact—their imagination and magical sense of what's possible. It's also a book about received wisdom, wisdom transmitted from generation to generation. The word *Kabbalah* refers to what is *received* (and we remember that receptivity is Leonard's Special Gift!). Transmission of learning and heritage through the generations is important here, but so is the simpler transmission of love and care between and among generations.

Reading Group Guide

1. Rachel Cantor's *A Highly Unlikely Scenario* has all the hallmarks of a traditional work of science fiction—time travel, a futuristic world, artificial intelligence. When you were reading *A Highly Unlikely Scenario*, did you feel like you were reading science fiction? Was there anything in the text that you were surprised to find in a science fiction novel?

2. Food is everywhere in this book. Leonard, the novel's protagonist, is "a good egg" (page 15) who works in the complaints department of Neetsa Pizza—a fast-food company that sells "pizza shaped according to Pythagorean principles" (page 9). His sister, Carol, makes "revolutionary stew" with "ingredients [that] remind us of our agrarian past" (pages 37–38). And the novel is populated by groups that identify themselves through food: "Survivalists wearing camouflage and offering samples of dried chipmunk; Heraclitan Grill flamethrowers in their characteristic fireproof togs; also, royal pages from the monarchists' Food Court, [and] barbecuties from the Whiggery Piggery (page 91)." What is the significance of food in Cantor's novel? Is food really at the center of the novel, or does Cantor use food as a vehicle for talking about ideas that are more central to the text?

3. What does it say about the world in which the novel is set that the legacies of many of history's most important mystics, theologians, and thinkers have been appropriated by a "parastatal corporation" (page 79) like Neetsa Pizza that uses their ideas as advertising tools? Do you think a statement is being made about the place of

spirituality and mysticism in our world? What do you think that statement might be?

4. The Brazen Head (which is based on stories of real automatons capable of answering any question) often seems like a more animated, opinionated version of Wikipedia. And it, like Wikipedia, proves in the end to have real people behind it, capable of making mistakes and having particular agendas. What do you think of sources that appear to be authoritative? Have you ever contributed to Wikipedia, and did that change your perception of it?

5. As the plot progresses, Leonard discovers that Felix, his nephew, has many special powers, including the ability to freeze time and read the writing in the never-before-deciphered Voynich manuscript. How do Felix's special powers change the nature of the relationship between Leonard and himself? And between himself and Sally?

6. Isaac the Blind's main aim in the book is to prevent mystical knowledge—such as the kind that Marco Polo and Roger Bacon learn about during their respective journeys—from getting into the wrong hands. Do you think that the circulation of knowledge can or should be restricted? Is there any knowledge that would be dangerous in the wrong hands?

7. One of the most important recurring images from the novel is that of the orchard. The orchard first appears on page 37, when Felix describes a dream he has had, where four men go into an orchard. What they see in there kills one, makes the second crazy, and turns the third into "a destabilizing force of chaos." Only the fourth man, described as the rabbi, is unaffected. When Leonard

and Sally encounter him in Rome, the Spanish mystic Abulafia claims to be "the rabbi who saw what was there and went home again" (page 230). Do you believe him? What do you think they see in the orchard?

8. How do you feel about the choice Sally makes in the end, passing up the chance to study with Abulafia for love, family, and becoming a leader in her own time? Would you make the same choice?

Food, mostly. Fast food. That's my business, fast food.

Fast food: I'm afraid the translation is poor.

Food one can obtain quickly, Leonard said.

As from a tavern? Mill asked.

Kind of.

And this makes your merchants rich?

I suppose so, Leonard said.

Mill was silent, as if absorbing this astonishing fact.

We are also known for our frocks, Leonard said. And our greatcoats.

I should like to see these marvels, Mill said. Perhaps I could trade them for amber. Or pepper.

Pepper?

And fauna? What manner of beast roams your countryside?

Leonard had to think again. Aside from Medusa, he'd not had much experience with beasts.

Chipmunks, he said. Apparently, we're overrun.

Chipmunks! Mill said. This beast is unknown to me! Are they cultivated by friars?

Mill laughed his low, wheezy laugh at this piece of inexplicable humor.

They have a stripe, Leonard explained. Down their back.

Excellent! Are they large and suitable for eating? Are they put to pasture? Are they captured through the hunt?

Leonard thought about this for a moment.

The Survivalists make a stew of them in their bunker cafés.

Wonderful! Mill said. Truly, you live in a fascinating land!

I guess so, Leonard said.

Are you a Jew? Marco asked.

I beg your pardon? Leonard asked.

I sense in your voice a trace of Mainz.

I have no religion, Leonard said.

Silence.

You are a Saracen, then? You worship Mahomet?

I don't believe in God, Leonard said.

Again, silence.

You are a Tartar, then? An idolater? A fire worshipper?

I have no religion, Leonard said. I worship nothing.

A silence so long, Leonard thought the line had gone dead.

I have seen many wonders, my friend, but none so strange as this. In Fu-chau, I met persons who were Christian and did not know it! I had to explain this most important fact to them! Papa insists they were Manichean. Whatever the case, at least they held some belief.

My family's Jewish, if that helps, Leonard said. My grandfather's grandfather was a rabbi.

Ah! You have been excommunicated. I am very sorry. I am a member of the true faith, of course, a devoted subject of Pope Boniface VIII.

Pope what?

You do not know Boniface? He is no more?

Leonard was astonished to hear Mill weep, and again allowed compassion to well. But then Mill said, It seems only yesterday Gregory named us official legates to the Great Khan—and Leonard didn't feel so bad.

And so it went: Mill calling several times a night, Leonard eventually communicating the concept of call queuing so he could excuse himself should a real call come through, which it did not. His phone logs continued to fill, he seemed even to be increasing his conversion rate, for which accomplishment NP sent him a semiprecious, metal-plated, equilateral calzone.

Leonard didn't mind talking with Mill, especially now that

his screen was acting so strange, with Sue & Susheela napping most of the time, the Brazen Head too (a note—*Out Fishin'*—taped to its head). When Mill called, those sites dissolved, crystallizing into diamonds scattered brilliant at the bottom of his screen—touching one, Leonard got an electric shock. Fifteen minutes after Mill's calls, his sites would crawl back, exhausted and ill formed. Sue & Susheela would be grumpy, the Brazen Head would blink stupidly and belch.

Leonard still hung up on Mill from time to time. When Mill called back, as always he would, he didn't seem bothered. In fact, he blamed himself.

Forgive me, he'd say. I learned much from the Tibetans, but I am no adept.

Then, invariably, the line would go dead.

Four men walk into an orchard

Six men with justice sticks came to Carol's house—the sound of their police caravans should have awakened Leonard, but it did not. Carol made Felix answer the door.

My mother is out planting flowers in honor of the Leader, Felix said. Would you like some claggum?

They took their treacle treats with them, and Carol pushed a clutchbag crammed with papers into the fire.

Records from my book group, she explained. Or so Felix said during his Time between Here and There. Which was getting longer every day. There was more and more Felix couldn't bring home—not just unkind classmates and ungraspable mathematical concepts, but hard-to-put-a-finger-on fears. To get through it all, they often needed to stop at the meeting rock in front of the municipal suggestion box.

Leonard wished he had more to offer.

Destabilizing forces of chaos have breached the walls, Felix said, sitting on the rock.

Impossible, Leonard said. The walls can't be breached. The Leader said so. He's an engineer, he should know.

Maybe, Felix said. Where do you think Mom goes when she goes to her book club?

She goes to her book club, Leonard said, though he'd often wondered the same. She's always been a big reader, he added.

Why aren't there any books in the house?

She uses the library, Leonard lied. Maybe she also reads at work.

You think Celeste hates me?

Sometimes people mistreat the ones they love.

I had a weird dream.

Oh?

It's very scary.

Leonard took Felix's hand.

Four men go into an orchard. Two are named Ben—that's the funny part—one is named the other one, and one is named Rabbi. Ben One sees something in the orchard that kills him; he's plucked apart by vultures while he's still alive.

That's terrible, Leonard said.

I know! Felix agreed. Ben Two looks around, and what he sees makes him crazy. The other one sees the same thing and turns into a destabilizing force of chaos. The only one who's not affected is Rabbi. He sees whatever it is and goes home just like he was.